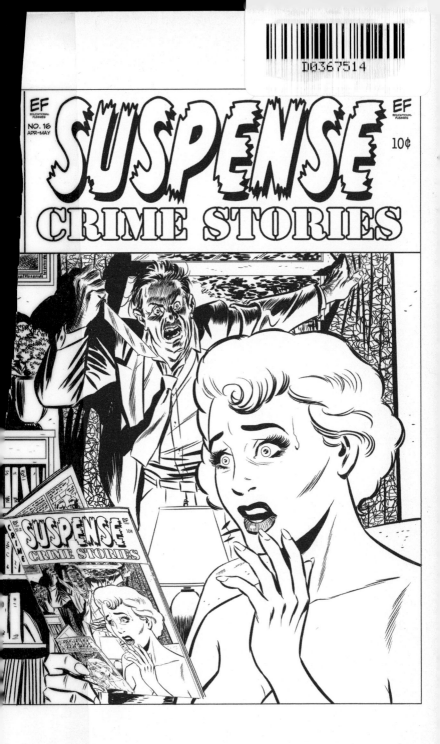

Raves For the Work of
MAX ALLAN COLLINS!

"Crime fiction aficionados are in for a treat...a neo-pulp noir classic."
>—*Chicago Tribune*

"No one can twist you through a maze with as much intensity and suspense as Max Allan Collins."
>—*Clive Cussler*

"Collins never misses a beat...All the stand-up pleasures of dime-store pulp with a beguiling level of complexity."
>—*Booklist*

"Collins has an outwardly artless style that conceals a great deal of art."
>—*New York Times Book Review*

"Max Allan Collins is the closest thing we have to a 21st century Mickey Spillane and...will please any fan of old-school, hardboiled crime fiction."
>—*This Week*

"A suspenseful, wild night's ride [from] one of the finest writers of crime fiction that the U.S. has produced."
>—*Book Reporter*

"This book is about as perfect a page turner as you'll find."
>—*Library Journal*

"Bristling with suspense and sexuality, this book is a welcome addition to the Hard Case Crime library."
>—*Publishers Weekly*

I went in and looked up the narrow flight of wooden stairs to the second-floor landing where, I'll be damned, there she stood.

She was, as the 25-cent paperback writers are wont to say, stark naked.

Stood there pale and white as the flesh of an orchid, her legs endless, her hips flaring, the waist narrow, breasts high and sweeping outward like a threat paid off by her dark erect nipples, a mane of gypsy curls brushing her shoulders.

She seemed poised to come down the steps, apparently in a hurry, her dark eyes so wide they were almost popping, and she was one step down when a second figure flew out onto the landing, a male figure, small, compact, wearing a t-shirt and rolled-up jeans and a face contorted with rage.

He shoved her hard from behind, like the guy on the cover of that Suspense Crime Stories *comic book at the hearing, and she was falling toward me as I hurtled up the stairs...*

SEDUCTION
of the
INNOCENT

by **Max Allan Collins**

INTERIOR ILLUSTRATIONS BY TERRY BEATTY

A HARD CASE CRIME NOVEL

A HARD CASE CRIME BOOK
(HCC-110)
First Hard Case Crime edition: February 2013

Published by

Titan Books
A division of Titan Publishing Group Ltd
144 Southwark Street
London
SE1 0UP

in collaboration with Winterfall LLC

Print Edition ISBN 978-0-85768-748-7
E-book ISBN 978-0-85768-749-4

Design direction by Max Phillips
www.maxphillips.net

Typeset by Swordsmith Productions

The name "Hard Case Crime" and the Hard Case Crime logo are trademarks of Winterfall LLC. Hard Case Crime books are selected and edited by Charles Ardai.

Printed in the United States of America

Visit us on the web at www.HardCaseCrime.com

For the real Seduction of the Innocent -
Bill Mumy
Miguel Ferrer
Steve Leialoha
Chris Christensen

"I am convinced that in some way or other the democratic process will assert itself and comic books will go."
DR. FREDRIC WERTHAM

"Most of my major disappointments have turned out to be blessings in disguise."
WILLIAM GAINES

SEDUCTION OF THE INNOCENT

Screw Hollywood.

In the spring of 1954, New York *is the entertainment capital of America.*

Sure, Hollywood has its movies, but lately it's been stealing its scripts from TV—dramatic stuff like Marty *and* 12 Angry Men, *comedies like* Visit to a Small Planet *and* No Time For Sergeants…all originally produced on live TV right here in Manhattan.

You know what they shoot out in Hollywood, for TV? Kiddie crap like The Lone Ranger *and* Cisco Kid. *Sure, there's the rarity like* Dragnet *or* I Love Lucy, *but for real quality TV, it's* Studio One, The Philco-Goodyear Playhouse, *and* The Hallmark Hall of Fame. *And for laughs, you got Uncle Miltie, Sid Caesar, and Jackie Gleason, then on Sunday night, so stiff he's hilarious, Ed Sullivan. Live television out of New York.*

Your morning starts with The Today Show *with Dave Garroway and your day ends with* The Tonight Show *with Steve Allen (local now, but heading for network this fall). In between you have game shows like* Beat the Clock *and* I've Got a Secret, *soap operas like* Love of Life *and* Guiding Light, *not to mention the news with Douglas Edwards (CBS), John Cameron Swayze (NBC), and John Charles Daly (ABC) …dawn till dusk, dusk to midnight, live broadcasts from New York rule the airwaves.*

Meanwhile, on the radio? Bob and Ray. Top that, California.

And where do the Hollywood producers look to find their next box-office bonanza? Broadway, where right now Can-Can, Picnic, *and* Tea and Sympathy *are playing at the Shubert, Music Box and 48th Street Theatre respectively. And over at the Brill Building, any popular song that doesn't come from a Broadway musical is getting pounded out on a piano by one tunesmith or another.*

When Broadway isn't providing grist for the Hollywood mill, the book publishing industry is. Do any of these ring a bell — The Robe, Battle Cry, From Here to Eternity? *All major publishing resides in Manhattan, from class acts like Knopf and Random House to paperback outfits like Pocket Books (reprints) and Fawcett (originals). All the rags about Hollywood movie stars are published out of Manhattan, too, and so are the big-time news mags,* Time, Life, Look.

Then there's that powerhouse publishing industry that nobody talks about, or anyway when they talk about it, it's either in hushed tones or outraged yells. No, I don't mean the skin magazines, though a lot of the guys in the biz I'm talking about started out there (and some still work sleaze as a sideline).

I am talking about funny books, kids.

The most popular entertainment medium of all, here in 1954. My city boasts twenty comics publishers putting out 600-some titles every month, selling eighty to one hundred million copies a week, reaching an audience larger than movies, TV, radio and magazines combined (they figure a comic book gets passed around or traded to six or more readers).

It's an industry employing a thousand-plus writers, artists, editors, letterers and assorted spear carriers, men and women, white and Negro and what-have-you. It's a form of story-telling that arrays newsstands with superhero fantasy and talking ducks, though those are outnumbered of late by monsters both supernatural and human, as well as cowboys and Indians, romance and war, and science fiction...even adaptations of classic literature ("Turn to page 345 in Great Expectations, *class—Timmy, that's page 16 in your* Classic Comics"). *The chief audience is kids but grown-ups indulge, too, especially veterans who learned to read portable funny books, bought at the PX, in the Second World War and more recently Korea.*

Me, I work in that industry, albeit on the fringes. My name is Jack Starr, and I'm the vice president of the Starr Syndicate, where that more respectable brand of comics is sold to news-papers nationwide—the comic strip. As it happens, Starr is, of the various syndicates, the one most closely aligned with the comic book industry. I'll tell you more about that in the pages to come, and about myself and my interesting boss, Maggie Starr, who happens to be my stepmother as well as the World's Second Most Famous Striptease Artist (after Gypsy Rose Lee) (retired).

What's important for you to keep in mind is how big, how popular the comic book industry is right now.

And how everybody and your Uncle Charlie wants to kill it. What the hell...every murder mystery needs a victim....

CHAPTER ONE

Speaking of live television, I had a stake in a local show on WNBC, *The Barray Soiree*. Not that Steve Allen or even Howdy Doody had much to worry about, but the show—airing 10:30 PM Monday nights, after the nationally aired *Robert Montgomery Presents*—was popular enough.

Harry Barray was a chatty disc jockey who made a mark doing on-air interviews with recording stars between platter spins. His NBT-FM radio show, *Sway with Barray*, had a decent following among borough-bound housewives taking a mid-afternoon beer or gin break.

Barray was alternately obnoxious and fawning—he was sort of Arthur Godfrey without the ukulele (or the talent)—and being even vaguely in business with this guy did nothing for my digestion.

Here's the thing. *The Barray Soiree* was what they called a "remote," a show broadcast not from a studio but a location. And Barray's weekly location was a big cushy corner booth of a popular Manhattan restaurant, the Strip Joint, just a block and a half off Broadway on Forty-Second Street. The bar took up the front third of the long, narrow space, with its tan plaster walls with dark wood trim and glass and chrome. This fed into the restaurant itself, tables and new comfy tufted booths replacing the original wooden ones.

Maggie Starr and I owned the Strip Joint, but that was really just an afterthought. We owned the whole building, six stories otherwise devoted to the Starr Newspaper Syndication Company, a couple floors of which were my quarters and Maggie's (hers on the fifth, mine on the third). A Chinese restaurant used to take up the main floor, but after Maggie found a fingernail in an egg roll, we reluctantly went into the restaurant business, more for her own dining convenience than an actual investment.

But the Strip Joint stayed solidly in the black, year after year, thanks to the chef Maggie imported from St. Louis and the simple, high-quality fare (best New York strip steak in, well, New York). The venue also benefitted from a wait staff consisting of gorgeous striptease artistes either between gigs or recently retired, a battalion of pulchritude in black tie, white shirt, and tuxedo pants.

Of course, more revealing looks at the lasses could be found in the bar area, where signed photos hung, usually as crooked as the leers of the male patrons studying them.

Elsewhere in the joint, comic strip characters rode the walls, courtesy of big-name cartoonists, encouraged by their usually absent hostess to contribute to the comic-strip ambience—mostly Starr Syndicate stuff, like Wonder Guy, Batwing and Mug O'Malley, but also Dick Tracy, Little Orphan Annie, and Alley Oop. Mostly these were grease-pencil drawings done right on the plaster, but the back wall had framed original comic-strip artwork.

The stripping theme, both burlesque and funny page, had come to attract two very different crowds—a luncheon two-martini businessman group, keen on the waitresses; and a suppertime tourist trade, from honeymooning couples to vacationing families, here to enjoy the renowned comic-strip wallpaper. Well, maybe the occasional Dad had snookered Mom into coming for the latter when the former was the real draw.

But what do I know about it? I'm a bachelor. Thirty-three, six feet erect (so to speak), dark blue eyes, dark brown hair, pulling down five figures with no yen to share it with a wife or kids or anybody else.

I'm the vice president of Starr, but my chief role is trouble-shooter—I look out for the syndicate's interests in the case of lawsuits, or when a cartoonist or columnist gets in a jam, or when a background check on prospective new talent is needed. This requires a private investigator's license, and the State of New York seems fine with getting my sixty-buck yearly fee.

Maggie was my late father's third and final showgirl wife. Major Simon Starr might have racked up more, but his heart attacked him before he could find a fourth showgirl to marry. If you're wondering why I didn't inherit the business, and why I wasn't the president of the Starr Syndicate, that makes two of us.

Not really. The major knew I was what they used to call a ne'er-do-well. I majored in drinking and coeds in college, and did such a fine job of it, I flunked the hell out. I was an MP during the war, and spent enough time wrestling drunks to not want to be one anymore. For nine years now I'd been on the wagon. But who's counting.

When the major made out his will, however, I was still a wastrel. There's a word you don't hear much anymore—still, till the Army straightened me out, that's what I was. So when my old man left the lion's share of his estate to Maggie, it came as no surprise. The only surprise was how effectively she moved from one kind of stripping to another.

Maggie, to tell you the truth, I felt not a whit of resentment toward. Even if she did own 75% of the Starr Syndicate (and this building and the Strip Joint) to my 25% (yeah, I know—who's counting).

She was a great boss, if not always as warm as the gawkers used to get in her audiences back in her striptease days. Funny thing about that name "Starr"—when she married the major, that had already been her stage name (her real last name was Spillman). Maybe the major had been attracted to her in part because she came with her own monogrammed luggage and towels. Maybe not.

My stepmother, who I lusted after only in my most out-of-control dreams, was not without eccentricities. She was, about half the time, a recluse. The Strip Joint even had a rear room she could sneak down to by way of her private elevator, and take meals when she was keeping out of the public eye.

Recently she had completed a six-month Broadway run as Libidia Von Stackpole in the musical version of Hal Rapp's comic strip *Tall Paul* (not one of ours) (damnit), and was still at or anyway near her "fighting weight" of 118. She had a fully outfitted gym just off her office up on the fifth floor, and worked hard to stay appealing, even if she was no longer peeling.

Whenever she got up around 125—she had been as high as 135, and believe me, there was nothing really wrong with a pound of it—she went into full recluse mode. Not a foot out of the Starr Building, with a very restricted list of business associates allowed to meet with her in the office.

My guess was, after six months of strictly maintaining fighting weight due to the Broadway stint, she would fall off the wagon and before long get "fat and sloppy" (you know— maybe 130).

Right now, though, she was maybe 120 at most, a stunning woman just past forty who might have been thirty. She'd have looked even younger if she didn't insist on her "full battle array," which is to say endless fake eyelashes, heavy makeup over her natural girlish freckles, and a red mouth that Marilyn Monroe might say was overdoing it.

Past all that paint, she was a green-eyed natural beauty with bee-stung lips perfect for the Clara Bow/Betty Boop era of her rise as a teenage ecdysiast from Council Bluffs, Iowa.

At the moment, while I half-stood, half-sat at a stool at the bar, working on a rum and Coke (without the rum), trying not to wrinkle my gray Botany 500, Maggie was answering a question posed by Harry Barray. Her red hair (its color unknown in nature, unless you considered Lucille Ball nature) was brushing her shoulders, and her midnight-blue gown was clingy with her full bosom nicely on display. Eat your heart out, Faye Emerson.

They were seated in that corner booth, and you could barely see them past the bulky TV camera. Heavy micro-phones—three of them—were positioned around the linen-covered table, Maggie's trademark red rose in a vase getting lost in the broadcast trappings. That extra mike indicated a third guest might be joining in.

But right now it was just Harry and Maggie.

Six months before, when the program began, the TV station had at its own expense wired the restaurant so that all the patrons—and tonight the Strip Joint was at least at its

150 capacity—could hear Barray and his guests during the live broadcast. These were not tourists, not on a Monday night, rather sophisticated, cliff-dwelling Manhattanites. And I fit right in.

"Yes," Maggie said, in a rich, throaty contralto Bacall might well envy, "I'm aware that comic books are a big controversy right now. But I'd remind you, Harry, that I'm in the comic *strip* business."

Barray, a big blond man with once-pleasant features that had assumed the puffy, acromegalic look of the heavy drinker, let out a cloud of cigarette smoke that Maggie politely backed away from. His nose, its redness concealed by pancake, seemed it might explode at any moment.

"But Maggie," the disc jockey said, "your syndicate—the Starr Syndicate—aren't you more closely associated with comic books than any other outfit in your field?"

He picked up a comic book with a particularly disgusting horror-themed cover from the prop pile resting nearby, and shook it at her like a warrant for her arrest.

Her smile seemed warm enough but I could feel the ice in those eyes as if it were clinking in my Coke.

"We syndicate *Wonder Guy*. The enthusiasm for supermen has faded somewhat, Harry, and not long ago we dropped a couple of the comic-book properties from our roster."

He tossed the horror comic back on the pile as if disposing of a dead rat. "*Batwing? Amazonia?*"

"That's right."

"Those are two fairly controversial titles."

"Are they? We never had any complaints from readers."

His mouth was wide and thick-lipped and his smile was

wet. "Well, Dr. Werner Frederick has stated…uh, you're *familiar* with the good doctor?"

She nodded.

"Dr. Frederick, in an excerpt from his forthcoming book, *Ravage the Lambs*, labels the *Batwing* strip as perverse, saying there's an unhealthy relationship between Batwing and Sparrow."

She smiled. I knew she was wishing she could ask him to be more specific, and embarrass his ass; but a show biz pro like Maggie knew better than that. You behaved yourself on TV. Otherwise you were blacklisted like all those Commies hiding under Senator McCarthy's bed.

She said, "Most parents would find that notion absurd, Harry. Like Wonder Guy, Batwing represents justice and fair play and even patriotism."

He flashed a sly smile. "Aren't you part *owner* of Americana Comics, Maggie?"

"My stepson Jack and I have some shares in the company. We wield no editorial influence."

"But you get first crack at syndicating comic strip versions of Americana features?"

"Yes. With *Amazonia*, like *Batwing*, we did not have a large enough list of subscribing newspapers to keep it going. I wish we could have, because it's one comic strip built around a strong, adventurous heroine, and I think young girls enjoy that, for a change."

"Well, Dr. Frederick doesn't agree." Barray's sly smile dissolved into a concerned fold in his pious mask. "He finds …and I apologize to my audience for my frankness, but the doctor *is* a scientist…*sado-masochistic* elements in *Amazonia*."

There were whips and chains in that strip, all right. Man, you did not want to get on the wrong side of that Amazonia doll.

"Harry, have you heard about the psychiatrist who was showing ink blot pictures to a patient, but when the psychiatrist asked the patient to tell him what he saw in those ink blots, the patient refused. 'Is there something wrong?' the psychiatrist asked. 'Don't look at me, doc!' the patient said. '*You're* the one showing the dirty pictures!'"

This got a nice laugh from the Strip Joint audience, and even the bloated Barray flashed a grin. Too bad Barray hadn't done his homework—*Amazonia* had been created by a shrink. That might've provided him with a nice comeback.

But all he could muster was, "Maybe some of the dangers the critics see in these comics *are* in the eye of the beholder. But you can't deny that this new trend of crime and horror is a disturbing one."

"Is it?"

"Is it disturbing, you mean?"

"No. Is it *new*? I seem to recall, as a young girl, going to see Boris Karloff in *Frankenstein* and Bela Lugosi in *Dracula* …but I turned out all right, I think."

This might not have been the best argument, since she'd also been stripping at Minsky's when she was a "young girl."

"And they teach Edgar Allan Poe in schools," she reminded the disc jockey. "James Cagney and Edward G. Robinson are both still livening up our movie screens, and no one's complaining. And isn't *Dragnet* on NBC?"

Letting out more cigarette smoke as if emitting steam, Barray said, "Dr. Frederick says these so-called 'crime doesn't pay' books use the capture or downfall of criminals as a means of glorifying violence and depravity."

Now Maggie frowned, a rarity because she fought wrinkles as hard as she did pounds.

"I'd rather not have to defend those books," she said, "or condemn them, either. It's outside the realm of the Starr Syndicate."

"Is it? Don't you syndicate *Crime Fighter* to a growing list of papers?"

This was starting to feel less like a friendly chat at the Strip Club—a soiree, remember—and more like an ambush. But Maggie didn't ambush easily.

"We do distribute *Crime Fighter*," she said. "The hero is a costumed character not unlike Batwing…but, Dr. Frederick will be pleased to learn, without a young male companion."

"Crime Fighter's sidekick is a monkey."

"That's right." She gave him a smile that was both wicked and flirtatious. "And if you find that objectionable, Harry, then maybe *you're* the one showing the dirty pictures."

What could Barray do but laugh good-naturedly at that?

But he seemed relieved to be able to tell the audience at home that he'd be "right back with Maggie Starr and another special guest," after the commercial.

I went over, moving past a light on a tripod and around the massive camera, managing not to bump into the crew or stumble over the heavy cables. I leaned in and spoke to Maggie while a young male production assistant used a soft cloth to dab away the disc jockey's sweat, a makeup girl waiting anxiously to touch up his makeup.

Whispering, I said, "You're gonna take this bout on points."

Barely audible, her smile frozen, she whispered back, "I wouldn't mind scoring a knockout. I've been set up."

"You're doing fine. You don't seem defensive at all."

"How do I look? Nobody's touching up *my* makeup."

"Naw, you're on your own. But you look swell. I liked that shrink joke. Nice job, cleaning it up."

"Thanks."

"Keep it light now."

She gave my hand a rare squeeze and I made my way back to the bar, where Benny the bartender had held my ringside stool for me.

Meanwhile, the "special guest" Barray had referred to was being escorted through the tangle of cables into the waiting seat in the booth next to Maggie. He was a little guy with full head of dark hair parted in the middle, making two swooping wings out of the halves. He had an untrimmed mustache and tweedy sportcoat over a sweater and shirt— he'd pay for that under those lights—and carried the vaguely rumpled, absentminded demeanor of a Greenwich Village intellectual.

Which was exactly what he was. That and a minor celebrity locally, a professional expert who turned up on radio and TV, his specialty "the popular arts." He would opine on the profundity of *Krazy Kat*, declare John Ford a "modern folklorist," and Benny Goodman a musical genius.

Didn't disagree with those views, but Lehman's pomposity made irritating stuff out of them.

"Your book *The Velvet Fist* came out last year," Barray (back on the air) was saying after introducing his new guest, "and you raised a lot of eyebrows."

"Yes," Lehman said, in a pinched, nasal voice, "and I even

fought successfully against the United States Postal Service in court, to protect my rights as a citizen and scholar."

"What was the fuss over, Garson?"

"My central *thesis* was the 'fuss'—that graphic violence in the popular arts runs rampant while governmental censorship focuses exclusively on the depiction of natural, biological activities."

Lehman knew not to use the word "sex" on the air.

Maggie, who was expected to just sit there and look swell and not interrupt, asked, "Are you recommending *more* censorship or *less* censorship?"

She seemed genuinely confused.

This threw the little man, and Barray had to pick up the slack, saying, "Well, now, Maggie, that may be a moot point …two separate bills—one designed to ban crime and horror comic books, the other to regulate their contents prior to publication—have already been passed by the New York legislature."

"That's right," Maggie said in her low purr, "and Governor Dewey vetoed both. He knew they were unconstitutional."

Finally Lehman chimed in: "Even so, a *United States* Senate hearing on comic books, as they relate to juvenile delinquency, is scheduled to begin later this week, right here in New York City, if you didn't know."

Maggie was shaking her head, casting the pair an I-pity-you-in-your-stupidity smile that I knew all too well.

"Really, gentleman," she said, "don't you realize that opening this door will invite censorship into all forms of entertainment?"

"Personally," Barray said, in his gravest radio-announcer voice, "I believe no man should be told by another what he is allowed to see."

Lehman seemed to take the host's pompous pronounce-
ment as a betrayal, bristling. "Tell *that* to those who consis-
tently ban material relating to human…"

He almost said "sexuality."

"…biology."

"With all due respect, Garson," the disc jockey said, "Dr.
Kinsey's favorite subject is not the issue here." He plucked the
horror comic off the pile again and waved it like a flag. "It's the
violent garbage being foisted upon the youth of our nation."

Now Lehman was back on board. "Absolutely! These
periodicals are the worst kind of swill—a garish hodgepodge
of clashing colors, atrocious artwork, moronic writing, all
printed on the cheapest pulp paper pennies can buy—a very
celebration of violence."

I bet he wanted to say "orgy."

Calm as still waters, Maggie said to Lehman, "And you
would censor that?"

"Well, *something* must be done."

"Yet you fought the post office over censoring *your* book."

He stuck his nose in the air and it twitched like a rabbit's.
"My book was not cheap violent trash, glorifying crime and
killing."

Wasn't killing a crime?

"Mr. Lehman," Maggie was saying, with a gracious veneer,
"I seem to recall you writing a letter on my behalf some years
ago."

The shaggy-haired intellectual swallowed, and his neck
reddened. He was lucky this new color TV hadn't hit the
local broadcasts.

"I, uh, am afraid I don't recall," he said.

She gestured to her lovely decolletage. "When I was

arrested, a, uh...*few* years ago...when Mayor LaGuardia shut down the burlesque houses and made my act illegal...you wrote a spirited defense of my art that appeared in several local papers...and, in greater detail, in an arts magazine you edited called *Erotique*."

The little guy's face was bright red now—sort of like Yosemite Sam after Daffy Duck really got his goat.

Before his guest could have a stroke, however, Barray got back on track: "We have laws that forbid the sale of tobacco to minors. Why then can't newsstand or candy store proprietors be held to a similar standard with these foul comic books? They should be stamped 'adult.' "

Maggie said, "Is that where you'd keep Mother Goose—under the counter? In the nursery rhyme, the farmer's wife cuts off the rat's tail with a butcher knife. That's fairly grisly. So is an old woman putting children in an oven."

"*She's right!*" a voice from the audience cried out.

Startled, Barray looked past the lights into the relative darkness of the restaurant as a figure in a black-leather jacket, t-shirt and jeans moved through like a shark in choppy waters.

I could see Barray thinking quickly—*do I have this guy tossed out? Or make him part of the circus?*

"We seem to have an opposing opinion," Barray said. "Speak up, sir, so our audience at home can hear you!"

Just beyond the cameras, the young guy—he was maybe twenty—stopped, breathing heavily. He clearly hadn't expected an invitation to speak. He had a hair-creamed black pompadour with sideburns, and was slender, almost skinny, the leather jacket giving him what little heft he had. But he was almost six foot and damn near as handsome as Brando in *The Wild One*, whose kid brother he might have been.

"I'm in the business! I'm an artist! You don't know what you're talking about!"

"Why don't you come on over and join us," the disc jockey said, his voice genial but with an edge. "I'm sure we'd like to be corrected if we're wrong."

Barray looked at Lehman, and said, "If you'd step out of the booth for a moment, Garson, we'll make room for this representative of the comic book trade."

Soon the artist who looked like a young hoodlum had taken Lehman's place, the little intellectual standing just off-camera, looking annoyed and almost hurt to have been trumped by an interloper.

"First, your name, sir?" Barray asked his sudden guest. "And what comic book company do you work for?"

"Will Allison," he said, suddenly shy on camera. If he'd spoken any softer, the microphones would've been out of luck. "I draw science-fiction stories for EF."

"Entertaining Funnies!" the host erupted, eyes glittering with the gold he'd struck.

"That's right," Allison said, sullen, defensive.

"Such a charming, wholesome name for a comic book line that includes..." And he reached for a fresh example from the stack nearby. "...*Tales from the Vault*, with a young woman being strangled by a walking, rotting corpse, and *Suspense Crime Stories*, which depicts a hanged man with his neck broken and...ladies and gentleman..."

He addressed the camera.

"...I can't show these to you in close-up. They are simply too disgusting."

Nervous, the young artist said, "I didn't draw those!"

"Oh, but the company you work for did *publish* them."

"Yes. But those are not intended for little kids."

"Big kids, then?"

"We have tons of older readers like that, working stiffs, and college kids, too."

"Really?" Barray shook the comic book as if trying to dispel dirt. "How heartening to know the leaders of tomorrow enjoy …literature. What do *you* draw, young man?"

"I adapted a series of Ray Bradbury stories for *Weird Fantastic Science*. He's a respected writer of science fiction!"

Maggie said, "Mr. Bradbury is indeed a very respected author. And I'm familiar with this young man's work, as well. He's a gifted illustrator."

"If so," Barray said, "then Mr. Allison is prostituting his talents working for Entertaining Funnies—perhaps the most reviled of all these comic book vultures. I risk no slander or libel in making that statement—I base it on the words of a scientist…Dr. Werner Frederick, in his new book, *Ravage the Lambs*."

Then the show was over, and Barray was all smiles where Maggie was concerned, ignoring the Allison kid, who shuffled away from the booth, stepping over cables and around the cameras, looking lost, and like he might cry.

He was walking right past me and I said, "Hey, Will."

The handsome kid paused and frowned at me. "Do I know you?"

I held out my hand. "Jack Starr. With the Starr Syndicate. That's my good-looking boss you were sitting next to."

Right now, in front of the booth, Maggie was having a discussion with Barray, and she was doing all the talking. My stepmother looked placid but I could tell she was taking that clown to the woodshed.

"I've heard of you," Allison said, shaking my hand, smiling shyly. Then he jerked a thumb toward the booth where technicians were tearing down. "It was nice of Mrs. Starr, defending me."

"Call her 'Miss Starr,' if you ever want any more favors out of her." I patted his shoulder. "You did all right up there, kid." That was a lie.

"Thanks. Somebody had to stick up for what we do."

"Comics are just the latest whipping boy. Used to be dime novels. Then it was pulp magazines. It'll be something else soon enough."

He nodded glumly but managed a smile. He said it was nice meeting me, then moved across the way to join a good-looking blonde girl about his age in a Peter Pan blouse with a scarf, shift skirt, bobby sox and saddle shoes. Maybe he got made a fool of tonight, but this kid was going home with something better than Barray or Lehman could ever wangle.

I hadn't noticed Maggie coming up. I heard her before I saw her—asking Benny to fix her a Horse's Neck (ginger ale, whiskey, lemon peel, some ice cubes, in a Collins glass).

"You straighten that prick out?" I asked.

"Barray?" she said, lifting her eyebrows an eighth of an inch, a big deal for her. "Yeah. Said if he ever sprang an on-air attack on me like that again, he and his show could find another restaurant to broadcast his bilge."

"Bilge, huh? Pretty rough."

"He's an ass."

"Why put up with him?" Knowing, but wanting to make her work a little.

"He builds business."

Here at the Strip Joint, she meant; but she wasn't leveling, not entirely.

"What you mean is," I said, "you like having a TV show you can guest on that's just a few floors down from your digs."

"Now you're calling me lazy."

"There must be another word for it, but I can't think of one right now."

Somebody else was moving toward us—Garson Lehman. She glanced at him as he planted himself before us, wearing what I will delicately term a shit-eating grin.

"I hope you don't mind a good little intellectual row, Miss Starr," he said in that nasal whine, which was even more irritating when he was trying to be nice.

"I don't mind a good give-and-take, Mr. Lehman."

"Please. Make it Garson."

She nodded, almost smiled. Then her eyes opened in a "something else I can do for you?" manner.

His smile twitched nervously under the shaggy mustache. "I, uh, just wanted to make sure you hadn't taken any great offense. I'm really such a huge admirer of yours."

"You made that clear in your defense of my art, years ago."

"Yes, I believe I did." He stuttered a nervous laugh. "I, uh, also…uh…wanted to make an *offer*. A proposal."

"This is so sudden." One eyebrow went up a whole quarter inch. Damn.

He raised his palms chest high in surrender. "Obviously—now is not the time or place for business…but it does follow from what we were so spiritedly discussing."

"Does it?"

He nodded vigorously. "As Mr. Barray said, your newspaper

syndicate is closely aligned with the comic book business. In this climate, that's something of a burden."

"My shoulders may not be broad, Mr. Lehman, but they can take it."

"Please—make it 'Garson.' And may I call you 'Maggie'?"

She said nothing.

He swallowed and said, "I believe you know that I have a considerable reputation as a scholar and commentator on the popular arts. I was at the forefront of the anti-comic book controversy—the first to write about the subject, in *The Velvet Fist*. You might say I paved the way for Dr. Frederick."

"Yes, you might."

"And the doctor graciously acknowledges that. You know, I helped him on *Ravage the Lambs*."

"Helped him how?"

His smile seemed nervous. "Well, chiefly research. He credits me in the acknowledgments."

Her eyes were like green marbles, cold, unblinking. "That must be gratifying. What is your point, Mr. Lehman?"

"My point is that if I were to do a weekly column for you …on the subject of the popular arts…perhaps beginning with a defense of comic *strips* as opposed to comic *books*… it would be *beneficial* to your position."

Something glittered in Maggie's green eyes. What was it? Rage? Amusement?

"We'd have the Garson Lehman stamp of approval," she said.

"Yes! It would be *implied*, but…yes. Might take some of the heat off."

This was like a guy who just set fire to your house offering you a nice cool glass of water. From your own tap.

"I'll think about that," she said.

He already had a business card palmed, it seemed, and he passed it to her, saying, "You can reach me there. That's my office. It's in the Village."

No. Really?

Then he shambled off, smiling, shrugging, even waving.

"What a schlemiel," I said.

"He researched for Kinsey, too, you know. He's a letch and a pornographer, using comics as a scapegoat."

"Everybody needs a hobby."

Her eyes narrowed. "Germ of something, though."

"He's a germ, all right."

"Not my meaning."

She turned toward the bar, slipped her perfect fanny onto a stool. Took a healthy sip of her Horse's Neck. "How long do you need to do a full background check?"

"Local?"

"Local."

"How full?"

"Thorough but not obsessive."

I shrugged. "Couple of days."

"Good. Do one."

"On who?"

"Whom."

"Whom, then?"

She sipped her Horse's Neck and smiled. "Dr. Werner Frederick. Is whom."

CHAPTER TWO

Maggie sat behind that big cherry-wood desk of hers—it was smaller than a fry-cook's griddle, but just—looking both businesslike and lovely. She wore a white-buttoned charcoal linen frock with a man-tailored top, only a man's arms wouldn't be bare. Her red hair was down, brushing her shoulders, her makeup subdued (though her mouth was as red as the rose in a vase near her blotter), and her hands were folded as if saying grace. Her desk, typically, obsessively neat, bore little stacks of letters, comics submissions, color proofs and columnist copy.

I had settled into the wine-colored leather chair across from her maybe thirty seconds ago, crossing my legs, angling myself casually, careful not to wrinkle my light Navy tropical suit with pale yellow shirt and blue-and-yellow patterned tie. We were waiting for her assistant Bryce to bring our standard Coke-on-ice for me and cream-laden coffee for Maggie. It was after lunch, about two o'clock, on Wednesday.

A quick geography lesson—the office had an Old Boys' Club look with dark rich wood paneling that hadn't been changed since the major remodeled in 1932. A parquet floor peeked out around an Oriental rug, a wall of bookshelves at left brimming with unread leather-bound classics that glowered snobbishly across at the opposite wall's tasteless array of big framed posters of Maggie's 1941 Broadway show (*Starr in Garters*), her three movies, and some gaudy burlesque placards, one with her billed over Abbott and Costello.

Various dark wood, seat-padded chairs lined either wall, for when her two visitor's chairs couldn't accommodate the traffic. Wooden filing cabinets jutted from the rear wall, overseen by a portrait of the major by James Montgomery Flagg, which stared across the long, narrow space at the full-figure pastel portrait of Herself in feathers-and-glitter by Rolf Armstrong that loomed over her behind the desk.

"Tell me about Dr. Frederick," she said, her hands still folded. She rarely took notes. Like me, she had a good memory.

"First," I said, "I'd like to know why you want to know about that joker."

Nothing registered on that pretty puss. "Does it matter?"

"You mean, you're the boss, so if you say jump, I say how high? No. You say jump, I say yeah, why? I mean, I'm probably gonna jump, but I am a partner in this enterprise."

The green eyes were hooded. "You are at that. With a specified role."

"Right. Which is help out with investigatory stuff when our syndicate faces lawsuit trouble, or other jams our talent gets into, or run background checks on potential new talent before signing 'em on."

"That describes your role well."

"It does, and checking on Dr. Frederick's background doesn't fit any of those...unless he's suing us. You sure as hell aren't considering hiring him to write a comic strip."

"You never know." She checked her wristwatch, a little silver thing with diamonds that cost her about what my Kaiser-Darrin convertible set me back. "After all, he'll be here in fifteen minutes." She smiled sweetly. Or anyway, that was her imitation of a sweet smile.

I jerked a thumb toward the chair next to me. "Dr. Werner Frederick? Will have his pinched butt right here next to me?"

"Unless he doesn't show. Tell me about him."

What the hell was she up to?

Well, she'd said jump, so I jumped.

"He's a German, born in Cologne a little before the turn of the century, naturalized as an American in '29. Studied medicine in Germany and knew Freud. He makes it sound like they worked together, but I didn't get any confirmation of that. But they knew each other."

She nodded. "His specialty, psychiatry."

"Yeah. Guess I skipped that. He's one of those guys showing the dirty ink-blot pictures. Anyway, he joined the staff of the psychiatric clinic at Johns Hopkins in Baltimore. In the early thirties, he directed the New York Court of General Sessions' psychiatric clinic, where all the nasty crooks got their heads shrunk courtesy of the taxpayers. He testified in court a lot, usually for the prosecution, obviously …but after he testified for Albert Fish's defense team, he either got fired or just moved on, into private practice."

"Albert Fish," she said distantly. "There's a noteworthy case."

"Yeah. The Brooklyn Vampire. Child rapist, mass murderer, cannibal, perfect for the crime comic books. Interesting that the doc stuck up for Fish, but wants the comics killed."

"But they executed Fish, anyway."

"Sing Sing. Regular Friday night Fish fry."

That got neither a smile nor disgust out of her. Can't blame a guy for trying.

"So," I said, "he went into private practice. He's a widower, no kids. He lives in the Waldorf Towers, practices out of an office in his suite, and as you might expect has a pretty high-class clientele."

"The Waldorf allows him to conduct business out of there?"

"Yeah. It's not like he's selling hot dogs or motorboats."

"Did you get a sense of his character?"

I shrugged. "He's something of a publicity hound—a lot of radio, TV, magazine stuff, relating to this forthcoming screed on comics. This *Ravage the Lambs* thing. A big excerpt ran in the *Ladies' Home Journal* and attracted a lot of attention, mostly positive. Parents are always glad to have something or somebody to blame for why their brats are brats."

She thought about that. Her green eyes, damn near un-blinking, were staring past me. At the major, maybe.

Then she said, "So he's famous? Household-name famous?"

"Close to it, at the moment anyway." I shifted in my seat. "Why *doesn't* he do a strip for us? He can psychoanalyze Mug O'Malley and Wonder Guy, right on the funny pages."

"You think he's a crank."

"He's one of those stuffed-shirt do-gooders who come along every now then—goes all the way back to Anthony Comstock, doesn't it?—who tries to control what other people can publish or read. And he's making a buck at it. Lots of bucks. Pop psychology trash."

"Don't hold back, Jack."

"Look, he does do some good work. He works pro bono with poor kids at a Harlem clinic, for example. He testified recently in that Brown versus Board of Education thing, talking about the negative impact segregation has on Negro youths. He's not all bad. But he's dangerous."

"To society?"

"To us!" I sat forward. "Maggie, two of the comic book outfits he's targeting are tied at the hip to Starr—Levinson Publications, with the *Crime Fighter* comic strip, and don't forget, we are just about to climb in bed with Entertaining Funnies, his favorite whipping boy."

We were in negotiations right now with EF's owner/publisher, Robert Price, to syndicate a strip based on his new, very successful comic book, *Craze*, which lampooned TV shows, comics and movies. The idea for the strip version was to do a color Sunday-only page that lampooned other comic strips, the way Hal Rapp took *Dick Tracy* on in his strip-within-a-strip, *Hawknose Harry*. Our sales force, feeling out prospective clients, considered it sure-fire.

The door at the rear of the office opened and a slender male figure in black turtleneck and slacks entered with a tray in hand bearing the Coke and coffee. This was Bryce, a handsome, trimly bearded former Broadway dancer of perhaps thirty, who ruled the little world of the reception area with its tucked-away kitchenette. When a busted ankle had ended his stage career, he got hired on by Maggie as her major domo, and was as loyal to Maggie as Tonto to the Lone Ranger.

He was also unashamedly flaming. Maybe he'd been reading those Batwing-and-Sparrow comic books.

He delivered the coffee to Maggie, waited for her to taste and test the warmth and cream content, got a nod from her when she had, then he placed the Coke glass on the waiting coaster, uninterested in any review from me on my beverage, then stood there vaguely petulant, like he was waiting for either a tip or an apology.

"What?" Maggie asked.

He spoke in a melodic second tenor; the melody at the moment was in a minor key. "That Dr. Frederick character is in the waiting area. He is, I believe, ten minutes early. Someone should inform him that being ten minutes *early* is as offensive as being ten minutes *late*."

I said, "Maybe you could wrangle a quickie shrink session out of him. Just ask him a few innocent questions and he'll never know he's been had."

Bryce's chin jerked upward. "He's the *last* person I'd allow inside here," he said, tapping his cranium. "He believes people like me are sick. That we are twisted perverts and should either be cured or institutionalized."

I shrugged. "What do you expect from a Nazi?"

That actually made Maggie smile a little, but she said to me, "Don't egg him on." Then to Bryce she said, "We'll take him off your hands. Send him in."

Bryce went out with his head still high, and his walk was similar to the bathing-suit competition contestants at the Miss America pageant, only more graceful.

"Would have been fun," I said, "to let those two spend a little more time together."

"You're mean," she said. But she was still smiling.

Dr. Frederick strode in, a tall, thin exclamation point of a man in his late fifties with white hair, wire-framed glasses and a crisp dark suit with striped red-and-white tie. He might have been a funeral director or a minister. His well-grooved face lived in a narrow, horsey oval, his eyes dark and small but alert, with a wedge of a nose Chester Gould might have drawn.

I found myself standing.

"Werner Frederick," he said with a curt nod, though of course he needed no identification. A distinct German accent turned "Werner" into "Verner." He moved past me to reach across the desk and shake hands with Maggie, who had not risen, then extended his hand to me, and we shook. His firm handshake stopped just short of showing off. I also got another curt nod, and half-expected him to click his heels together.

I gestured to the visitor's chair, the mate of mine, and he sat, feet on the floor, arms folded, chin as high as Bryce's on the latter's exit.

"Thank you for accepting my invitation," Maggie said. "May I order up some coffee for you?"

"Thank you, no. I confess I am here more out of curiosity than anything. I am as prey to that human frailty as any layman."

I wanted to point out that curiosity wasn't exactly a frailty, but this was Maggie's show. I settled back comfortably and sipped my glass of Coke—Bryce had squeezed a lime in, bless him—and listened.

"I hope we're not adversaries," Maggie said. "But we are obviously on opposite sides of this comic-book controversy."

He shrugged his narrow shoulders. "That fact, of course, fuels my interest. As it happens, I caught that broadcast Monday night, when you and that television host and my friend Lehman got into your heated discussion." His smile was a thin line that curled at either end, patronizing but genuine. "I must admit, it made good viewing. I was amused by your comparison of comic books to traditional children's fairy tales."

She shrugged. "I believe it to be apt."

"With all due respect, Miss Starr, I certainly don't. Or is 'Mrs.' your preference?"

"Professionally, it's 'Miss.' And surely you can't deny, Doctor, that children's literature has always been violent. There's the grimness of the Grimm Brothers, *Peter Rabbit*'s farmer with a shotgun, *Peter Pan*'s pirates."

"Yeah," I said, not able to resist, "and what about those talking clams in *Alice in Wonderland* that got eaten up? Maybe your buddy Albert Fish read *that* as a kid."

Maggie flashed me a look that only I could read, but the shrink merely smiled. "You've read up on me, Mr. Starr."

"Part of my job around here, research. I'm clearly not the brains."

That amused him, just a little. He was taking no offense, I'll give him that much.

"I think all of us," he said, "prize the books we read and loved as children. Why, many of us save and even cherish the worn volumes themselves, those frayed mementoes of our youth, and carry them with us into adulthood."

He was right. I had still had the copies of *Spicy Models*, published by the major, that I'd lifted from his editorial offices when I was in the seventh grade.

"But it's hard even to imagine, isn't it," he went on, in his thick accent and perfect English, "any adult or even adolescent who has outgrown comic books ever *dreaming* of keeping any of those garish pamphlets over time, out of sentiment or any other reason."

He might have been wrong about that. My *Dick Tracy*, *Dan Dunn* and *Secret Agent X-9* Big Little Books were in my closet on a shelf. Next to the stack of *Spicy Models*.

"Be that as it may," Maggie said, "many comic books are perfectly harmless. Or do you object to the likes of *Donald Duck* or *Little Lulu*?"

"Such trash is less harmful than the crime comic books," he allowed. "I'm afraid the combination of simple text and crude pictures serves only to discourage children from reading *real* books. Inhibits their imagination. Still, the sale of such material, I don't protest."

I said, "But don't you lump the superhero-type of book in with the crime comics?"

He nodded. "I do." His eyes met Maggie's. "And this is what, I'm afraid, does indeed make us adversaries of sorts. Your syndication service has distributed the comic strip versions of some of the most dangerous of these characters."

Dangerous. That word again.

"The undercurrent of homosexuality in the *Batwing* comic book," he said as if tasting something sour, "is extremely damaging to impressionable minds, and children are inherently in that category."

"Homosexual?" I asked.

That got me another flash of a look from Maggie.

"*Impressionable*," he said sternly. "And the *Amazonia* comic book is rife with fetishistic bondage, and the lead character herself is *clearly* lesbian."

"She has a boyfriend, doesn't she?" I asked innocently. "Some captain in the army or air force?"

"Amazonia is a closeted lesbian, frequently shown participating in semi-clothed frolicking with other lesbians."

I never get invited to the good parties.

Rather than argue the point, Maggie said, "We no longer distribute those strips."

"That's an admirable decision."

I noticed Maggie didn't point out to him that in both cases that was a *business* decision.

"However," the shrink said, "you continue to distribute the strip version of one of the most offensive of these characters—Wonder Guy."

What the hell was offensive about Wonder Guy? He was just a big lug wearing patriotic colors and a cape, going around saving people from fires and earthquakes and punching out the occasional bad guy.

"This," he was saying, his eyes cold and glittering, lost in themselves, "is a reprehensible exhibition of the Nazi theme of the superman. A dangerous celebration of the triumph of power and violence over the logical and intellectual."

I wanted to point out to this dope that the creators of Wonder Guy were Jews, kids from Des Moines who came to the big city. Where *other* Jews screwed them, but that's another story.

"We also distribute," Maggie said pleasantly, putting it right out there, "the *Crime Fighter* strip, a spin-off of a very successful comic-book title. That puts us in business with Levinson Publications, whose output you hold in much disfavor."

"Yes," he said, but now his eyes were narrowing. *What is she getting at?* he seemed to be wondering.

What is she getting at? I was wondering.

"Here's what I'm getting at," Maggie said. "We are a syndication service, as you accurately put it. We provide content to over two thousand newspapers, Sunday and daily. Some of those papers editorially are Republican, others are

Democrat. A good number are in major cities, but many more are in small towns."

"Yours," he granted, "is an egalitarian pursuit. But I'm not sure I understand *how* that explains..."

She raised a palm like a traffic cop. "We have comic strips that appeal to young children, and we have comic strips that appeal to teenagers, with soap-opera strips for women, a sports strip for dads, and panel cartoons for both sexes."

He had begun shaking his head perhaps halfway through that. "I have no objection to comic strips *per se*. They are an established medium in the pages of our newspapers. The controversy, so-called, over the crime comic books does not apply, generally, to the comic strip."

"I assure you that comic strips, back at the turn of the century when they began, were crude and rude, fodder for the lower-class, for immigrants, and got plenty of criticism. *The Yellow Kid* was a hoodlum, the Katzenjammer Kids juvenile delinquents."

The doctor was frowning. In thought, maybe. Or maybe not.

"I do not dispute that the comic strip," he said, mildly irritated, "has blossomed in its limited way in the greater garden of the American newspaper. But its bastard child the comic book is a poisonous weed that infests our newsstands. A dozen state legislatures have worked to ban or limit this blight upon our children, and many parents have risen up, even having public burnings of these wretched pamphlets."

And here I thought the doc didn't *like* the Nazis....

Maggie raised her hands as if in surrender. "I didn't invite you here to argue, doctor. But I did want to...clear the air."

From his seat he bestowed her a little quarter bow. "I never mind discussing this or any topic with a person of your intelligence."

"Nice to know." She rocked back in her swivel chair. "I needed to find out if our disagreement on this subject would stand in the way of our doing business."

This clearly surprised him. "Business? Of what kind?"

Now she sat forward and her tone became strictly professional. "We're in the market for a self-help column, doctor, somewhat in the fashion of *Dear Abby* or *Ann Landers*."

Oh, she was good....

The doc's eyes were wide as his integrity, ego and greed began an epic battle (integrity seemed outnumbered). "That's hardly my calling, Miss Starr...."

She flipped a hand. "The kind of questions asked and answered in those columns by these self-appointed experts... did you know Abby and Ann are sisters, and quite hate each other?...are of a rather tepid and ordinary nature."

"From what I've seen, I would agree."

"We at Starr believe that a column written by a psychiatrist, particularly a prominent, well-respected one, could be genuinely helpful to readers...*and* financially rewarding to columnist and syndicate."

I liked that "We at Starr" thing. Made me feel part of a team.

The doc was saying, "It would perhaps be unethical for me to treat a patient through an advice column...."

"You wouldn't treat patients, nor would you handle any problems that couldn't be simply answered with good common sense, enhanced by your impressive training as a doctor of the mind. For someone with a serious problem, you would recommend treatment by a fully accredited psychiatrist."

"I see." He looked like a twelve-year-old who'd just been told the facts of life and was appalled yet intrigued. "Well, that *is* an interesting notion...."

I gave Maggie a look that said: *He's hooked—reel him in.*

"Think of what you would do, doctor, for the science of psychiatry! Think of the millions of readers, many of whom are afraid of 'head shrinkers,' coming into daily positive contact with a kind, gentle, brilliant practitioner of the art."

I was afraid she was piling it on a little too high, but Frederick was caught up. He was sitting on the edge of his chair, his eyes wide and glittering, like a kid racing to the end of a horror comic.

"You make a good case for this cause," he said.

Already his ego and greed had convinced his integrity that doing a syndicated column was a "cause."

"But," he cautioned, waggling a professorial finger, "I have commitments that might prohibit my taking this offer.... Could it be a *weekly* column?"

Well, she had him. He was flopping around the deck, unaware he was heading for the taxidermist and the cabin wall right over the fireplace.

"I have my private practice to consider," he went on, "my duties at the Harlem clinic, and right now, of course, I'm promoting my new book...and I'm thinking of doing a follow-up, on the harmful effect of TV on young minds...."

I had told Will Allison comic books were only the latest whipping boy. Here comes TV as the next parental boogey-man!

"If you like," Maggie said, "we could find an assistant for you..."

A ghost, she meant.

"…someone who could deal with the many letters we'd receive daily, winnowing them into material for columns, and writing first-draft for you to revise and approve. You might only have to work on the column a few hours per week. And you would make five figures, easily, and more likely six."

Judging by his expression, he might have been Long John Silver viewing a treasure chest heaped with gleaming doubloons. "I could make as much as $100,000 a year for performing this service?"

"Our top cartoonists make many times that." She clasped her hands with a clap. "What do you say? Will you consider it?"

He was nodding like I did the night Betty Jean Willis asked me if I wanted her to climb into the backseat of my Chevy.

"I will," he burbled. He actually burbled. "I'd want to meet and approve and interview any potential assistant, naturally."

"Naturally."

"Would I be under any constraints?"

"Well, of course, we would hold back the names of anyone writing in—that's where 'Frustrated in Queens' and 'Lonely in Dallas' comes in. You'd have the usual legal and moral restraints. You'd have to avoid, or handle very delicately, any sexual topics."

"Certainly."

"And obviously I would ask that you refrain from any discussion of comic books or strips in the column."

There it was—the cherry on her sundae, the worm in his apple.

"But that's what I am best known for," he said.

Her nod was matter of fact. "It is, but you have your book and your personal appearances for that. And this column will broaden your appeal, and present you as not just a one-note authority, but…well, if all goes as I see it, you'd be 'America's Psychiatrist.' "

His eyes were playing the Star-Spangled Banner. He listened to it and we just watched him.

Finally Maggie said casually, "Anyway, with the Starr Syndicate's peripheral involvement with comic books… specifically the strips we run that are spin-offs of such publications…it would be something of a conflict of interest for you to wage that war in *our* pages."

"There are other places for that," he said.

Rest in peace, integrity. Take your bows, ego, greed.

"Good," Maggie said, smiled big and slapped the table with her hands.

The doc jumped a little. But he then understood that he'd been dismissed, getting to his feet, asking, "What's the next step?"

"Our lawyers will write up a contract for you to show your lawyers."

Which would include language banning him from discussing comics, and making the assistant's salary his responsibility.

"All right," he said, dazed but smiling.

She reached her hand out and he shook it. He nodded, bid her several goodbyes, did not shake my hand (he'd forgotten all about me), and loped out, with the gait of a man who'd just narrowly missed getting hit by a bus—relieved but unsteady.

Only he *had* been hit by a bus.

I said, "You are a very evil woman, and I admire you for it."

Pleased with herself, Maggie said, "You are too kind."

A few moments later, Bryce stuck his head in. "I thought he'd *never* leave!...Look, I've got Bob Price out here, hiding in the kitchenette!"

The owner/publisher of Entertaining Funnies.

Maggie snapped, "Did he and Frederick *see* each other?"

"No! But I slipped up and told him Frederick was meeting with you, and it was all I could do, keeping him from running in there and *strangling* that quack!...Should I send him in, or wait till he has a stroke?"

CHAPTER THREE

As if exiting a burning building, Robert Price came bounding into the office, brushing past Bryce holding open the door. Bryce shut us in with a heavenward glance as the Entertaining Funnies publisher all but ran to the chair Dr. Frederick had so recently vacated. When he reached it, the big man paused, as if he could see Banquo's ghost sitting there.

Dark-haired, with a big oblong head, eyes small and bright behind black-rimmed glasses, Price wasn't much past thirty, a heavyset guy not exactly fat, a six-foot heavyset force of nature even when he wasn't pissed off, red-and-blue geometric-design tie flapping like the flag of a foreign nation. His tan slacks were flapping, too, like there was a high wind in Maggie's windowless office. Sans suit coat or sports jacket, in just a short-sleeved white shirt with tie, he might have been a high school chemistry teacher.

Which had been his ambition, till his father died in a boating accident, leaving him Entertaining Funnies to run.

Price's father Leo had been part of the quartet of entrepreneurs that included the major, Donny Harrison, and Louis Cohn, who developed the first comic books, which had led to Americana Comics, lucrative home of *Wonder Guy* and *Batwing*. They had started out printing Yiddish newspapers, expanded into racing forms and finally smut, the latter nothing so creative as this kid Hefner was currently was turning out—just rags filled with semi-clothed pics of strippers and showgirls, emphasis on the semi.

There was general disagreement over which of the quartet got the idea to format comic-strip submissions into pamphlets for giveaway purposes with various products. But everybody agreed it was Leo Price who had slapped "Ten Cents" stickers on the covers of the extra copies, distributing them to newsstands and accidentally creating the comic-book medium.

Harrison and Cohn came to control Americana Comics, while the major wound up with Starr Syndicate and a piece of Americana. Price sold out his share in the latter to start his own comics line, Entertaining Funnies.

Well, originally it had been Educational Funnies. Leo wanted to class up the comics business, finding Americana's long-john heroes distasteful. Instead he published comic books illustrating Bible stories, as well as a secondary kiddie line (which is where the "Entertaining" designation came in) with a singularly non-stellar line-up—*Jim Dandy*, *Animal Tales*, *Fable Fun*. All of those bled money, and when Leo died, this four-color albatross wound up around his unassuming son Bob's neck.

Initially Bob Price would just stop by to pick up his paycheck, but when Entertaining Funnies appeared on the verge of bankruptcy, the reluctant funny-book publisher started actually publishing. He brought on talented artist/writer/editor Hal Feldman, fresh off *Archie* knock-offs that had featured big-busted Betty and Veronica imitations (Dr. Frederick liked to call these "headlights" comics). For a year or so, the new team followed comic-book trends, western, romance, crime, before stumbling onto horror out of their mutual love for scary old radio shows like *Lights Out* and *Inner Sanctum*.

Feldman assembled some of the best artists in the business, who in grisly detail depicted horrors that radio would consign to its listeners' imaginations—bloodthirsty vampires, flesh-tearing werewolves, drooling ghouls, and desiccated zombies. Their science fiction comics were variations on the terror theme—grotesque monsters attacking spacemen—and their crime comics dropped "true crime" in favor of greed-and-sex sagas, husbands killing cheating wives, wives killing fat old rich husbands.

And Bob Price had gone from unassuming aspiring high school teacher to enthusiastic, high-energy comic book czar.

That czar was standing there—his tie had settled down but he hadn't—pointing a finger at the vacant chair next to me.

"He was sitting right there!" Price said, eyes popping behind the glasses, veins standing out on his forehead. "You had that monster sitting right *there!*"

"Yeah," I said. "All warmed up for you."

"Maggie," Price said, his voice trembling with hurt, "how *could* you?"

He sounded like the disappointed villainess at the end of *I, the Jury.*

Maggie, hands on her desk folded, smiled politely. Now she was the one who seemed like a schoolteacher. "Bob—what a nice surprise, you dropping by. Please sit down."

"I can't bring myself to!"

I said, "You want me to go downstairs to the restaurant and get you one of those tissue-paper dealy-bobs they use in public toilets?"

He swung his gaze on me. We were friends, or anyway

friendly acquaintances, going back well before he became a comic-book publisher. The major and his father had been business partners, after all.

And my absurdly sarcastic question made him break out into a grin and he started to laugh, and plopped himself down in that accursed chair. He sat forward, though, hands together between splayed legs.

"But come on, Maggie," he said, shaking his big head. "What were you doing fraternizing with the enemy?"

"I'm trying to make him *less* an adversary," she said. She pointedly avoided calling Dr. Frederick "the enemy."

His eyebrows climbed. "How is that *possible*?"

I glanced at Maggie and she nodded, and I said, "We offered him a syndicated column with Starr."

He had the shocked expression of a kid who just read the last panel of a *Tales from the Vault* horror yarn.

"We offered him an advice column," she said. "A psychiatric spin on *Dear Abby*. And he has said yes, at least tentatively."

Price's eyes brightened, like a jack-o-lantern whose candle had just been lit, and he began to smile. The effect was not unlike a jack-o-lantern, either. He pointed a waggling finger at her. "You are a *genius*, Maggie Starr. An outright goddamn genius. You appealed to that outsize ego of his, and bought the son of a bitch off, without him even knowing it!"

She raised a cautionary hand. "I wouldn't put it quite that way…"

"Of *course* you wouldn't!"

"…but it does potentially put the good doctor in an awkward position. He will find himself working for a firm that is financially tied to Americana Comics, and of course Starr has a history with you and your family as well, so…there are those who would interpret him as, I believe the Madison Avenue term is, selling out."

Bob was laughing now, so hard he was crying. He dug out a hanky and dabbed his eyes with it and blew his nose with a honk.

I said, "It's going to be in his contract that he can't discuss comic books or even comic strips in his column."

Still laughing, Price put the hanky away and said, "Beautiful. So beautifully played. You'll show everybody what a *hypocrite* he is."

Maggie frowned thoughtfully. "*Is* he a hypocrite? He appears sincere."

Price pawed the air. "Oh, he's a hypocrite, all right. I've just come from my lawyers. We got an advance copy of this anti-comics *Mein Kampf* of his—*Ravage the Lambs*? He fills it with examples of panels from the comic books he criticizes, the most extreme and outlandish out-of-context stuff he could find. You know that story we ran about the midnight football team?"

"I missed that one," I said.

"Well, the last panel reveals that they've been playing not with a football, but with their hated coach's head."

"Ah. And that final panel is what Frederick used."

"That's right. Wholly out of context! One of Craig Johnson's *Postman Always Rings Twice* variations, where the husband strangles the wife? Guess what panel that bastard uses!"

"Where the husband," I said, "is strangling his wife?"

"Bingo! Fills this 'anti-violence' book of his with the most violent images he can lay his grubby hands on. He's exploiting comics to make a buck, far more than any comic book ever exploited anything or anybody!"

Maggie said, "Why were you at your lawyers, Bob?"

His grin was again Halloween-worthy. "That dippy doc never bothered getting permission to excerpt those panels. That's copyrighted material, Maggie! I'm gonna sue his pants off. Then I'm gonna sue his *ass* off."

Thoughtfully, Maggie said, "Because it's a scientific work, those examples from your publications *may* be fair use."

He pawed at the air. "That's what my legal guys are looking into. But they think we may have a case, because this isn't *really* a scientific work, not the way he's promoting it on radio and TV, and selling excerpts to *Reader's Digest*, *Parents* and *Ladies' Home Journal*."

I glanced at Maggie. "Bob has a point. The doc's going the pop psychology route. I mean, most scientific treatises aren't called *Ravage the Lambs*."

She didn't react to that, turning to her guest, moving on to a new topic. "Bob, why did you stop by? You didn't come to complain about Frederick coming to see us—you didn't even know about it."

The big man leaned back in the chair and loosened his tie; it wasn't particularly warm in the office but he was perspiring, and his white shirt had the sweat circles to prove it.

"You're right," he said, "but this *is* about Frederick, partly. You know tomorrow's the first day of the Senate hearing over at the Foley Square Courthouse."

Maggie and I nodded. The papers had been giving this investigation into juvenile delinquency and comic books a lot of play.

"Well," Price went on, "Frederick is the first witness scheduled, and guess who the *second* witness is?"

Maggie winced. "You were *subpoenaed*?"

"No! I volunteered."

I winced. "Why the hell?"

He threw his hands up. "To state my *side* of it. I've been up for two days and nights working on my opening statement."

He did seem wired. Dexies?

In any case, his eyes were as wide and wild as Caligula asking his sister out for a date. "I'm going to put that hypocritical head-shrinker in his goddamn place! And I'm going to educate those so-called lawmakers on the ins and outs of the great American right of free speech."

"Yeah," I said. "That worked out swell for the Hollywood Ten."

"I'm no communist!"

"No, Bob," I said, "you're worse. You're despoiling America's beloved boys and girls. You're the comic-book equivalent of the pervert offering candy to kids at the schoolyard fence, next to the guy selling them dope."

He was shaking his head. "I know all about the garbage that prudes like Frederick and Lehman have been stirring up about me. That's why I'm taking the stand. When I'm finished, everyone will know what I am."

A fool?

"I am a *publisher*." His chin jutted.

Probably the guy who said he regretted having only one life to give for his country had a chin that jutted just like that—made it easier to slip the rope around.

"My opening statement will be a masterpiece. I need to work on it some more, but…it's going to turn this *whole* thing around."

Maggie said, "You volunteered to be a witness. Can you get out of it?"

"I don't *want* to get out of it!"

"You should," she said sternly. "I can arrange for some major newspaper to interview you, maybe get you on a television show more friendly to the Bill of Rights than *The Barray Soiree*. Steve Allen, possibly. You can get your side of it out much better that way."

"No! The battle lines are drawn. It's me against them, and they don't stand a chance."

"Ever hear of the Alamo, Bob?" I asked.

"In the *end*, the Forces of Right won, didn't they?"

"If you mean the Mexicans, yeah."

But he wasn't having any of it. He shook his big head rather woefully, sweat flecking off his Brylcreemed locks. "Look, I *know* this is dangerous."

Dangerous—the word Dr. Frederick so often used about comic books like the ones Bob published....

"Jesus," he said resignedly, "lately I get more death threats than Joe DiMaggio!"

Maggie asked, "Why does Joe DiMaggio get death threats?"

"He married Marilyn Monroe!" He sat forward again and gestured with open hands, something pleading in his tone, and I hoped this wasn't how he planned to testify. "Look, Maggie, Jack...I didn't come up here to get your permission or even explain why I feel I have to do this thing. But I *do* need your *help*."

Maggie and I exchanged glances. Price was bringing the *Craze* comic strip to us, and despite all the criticism Entertaining Funnies had received, we knew this particular property was a potential goldmine.

So she said, "How can we help?"

His grin was more school kid than chemistry teacher. "I'd

like Jack here to accompany me to the courtroom, and play bodyguard."

I frowned at him. "I'm pretty sure there'll be cops around at that courthouse."

He shook his head, the grin gone. "No, I need somebody to babysit me but good. From my office to the street, from the street to that courthouse, and back out again. There's violence in the air. There are reporters that need keeping back. Jack, will you do that?"

I glanced at Maggie, who gave me a barely perceptible nod.

"Sure," I said. "You just let me know what time and I'll meet you over at your office."

He grinned in relief and leaned over and offered me a hand to shake, which I did, as he said, "Thanks, Jack. Thanks, man."

Price seemed about to rise when Maggie asked a question: "Did you see the broadcast from the Strip Joint Sunday night?"

"You bet I did. I try not to miss any appearance by Frederick or his puppet, that clown Lehman. Talk about hypocrites! That Lehman's a pornographer!"

"People in glass houses," I said, "shouldn't throw horse apples. Your pop and the major co-published plenty of sleaze in their day."

Price patted the air. "Okay, okay. No argument." He smiled at Maggie. "Look, I really appreciate the way you stuck up for us comic book guys. Not a popular position."

Maggie nodded a curt thanks, then said, "I wanted to ask you about this boy, Will Allison. I was afraid things might come to blows between him and Harry and that Lehman character the other night. I have a feeling only his natural shyness, once on camera, prevented a really unpleasant scene."

Price was nodding. "Will's an impulsive kid. Something of a hothead, frankly. But what a talent. He could be the next Hal Foster."

"I've seen his work," Maggie said, her tone appreciative. "I'd like to keep an eye on him for the future. But if he's not *stable*...."

Price waved that off. "He's just young and kind of... fragile. Handsome kid but out of step. I've tried to help him out. I'm even paying for sessions with my shrink."

"What?" I said. "With Dr. Frederick?"

"Yeah, right! Naw, with a great little gal down in the Village, Sylvia Winters. She's tops and you'd like her, Jack. Cross between Kim Novak and Grace Kelly."

That sounded promising. Maybe I could whip up a neurosis.

Price rose, thanked us both, told me he'd call with details about tomorrow, shook our hands, and went out.

I was getting up, too, thinking this session was over, when Maggie said, "I want you to look this Dr. Winters up. She's probably in the book."

"Probably. Why?"

"I'm a little worried about Bob."

"You mean, he looks like he hasn't slept for days, yet is feeling no pain? Like popping pills, maybe?"

"He's high-strung all right. See what Dr. Winters' opinion is about him testifying."

"She's a doctor. There are privacy issues."

"She's a woman. And you're a charming devil."

Was that sarcasm? I couldn't always tell with her.

"And while you're at it," she was saying, "see if she'll provide any insights about Will Allison. I'd like to know if he's got problems that would preclude us hiring him on to do some work."

"You have something in mind for him?"

She nodded. "Thinking about developing a science-fiction strip. You know, the Allison boy draws like a young Ray Alexander."

Alexander created *Crash Landon*, the top sci-fi strip, or it had been till he quit to draw a private eye feature called *Nick Steele*. Some said I'd been Alexander's inspiration for the latter.

Maybe that would impress this Winters dame. You know, when I was charming her.

I rose. "This is just a plan to get me next to a psychiatrist, isn't it?"

"With your ego," she said pleasantly, "a little head shrinking couldn't hurt. Now run along."

As long as I can remember, Greenwich Village—that fabled artsy section belting the city below 14th Street—has been home to cafes, coffee houses and hideaways, and even the occasional actual nightclub. Seemed all it took to open up a Village spot was a vacant storefront or cellar, a few thrift-shop tables, some empty bottles to stick candles in, some filled bottles of wine, an espresso machine, and a beat-up piano (preferably in tune).

Considered by some the hippest cabaret in all New York City, the Village Gateway on Thompson took up a hotel basement just off Bleecker Street. Soon a crowd would be lined up to get in—this was jazz night (folk music and poetry readings alternated on the others) and Charlie Mingus would be going on around ten. But I was even earlier than the tourists—I strolled into the big low-ceilinged room just after five.

Though the Gateway wasn't the intimate hole-in-the-wall of a genuine GV retreat (that's Greenwich Village, for the squares among you), the atmosphere was just right—scuffed round wooden tables, walls with murals and sketches drawn right on, like the comic-strip doodles at the Strip Joint, but with less artistry, in my book. Right now the cavernous space held only a handful of patrons, mostly angry, edgy young poets of both sexes—you'd be angry and edgy, too, if you'd been drinking espresso all day.

Dr. Sylvia Winters was a cut above the other females in the Gateway, with their long black hair and no makeup and lip-drooped cigarettes. Still, she fit right in, in the black, bulky yet oddly form-fitting sweater with tight black pants. She had a short platinum-blonde hairdo with a sharp comma of curl framing her face on one side, and that beautiful mixture of Kim Novak and Grace Kelly that Bob Price promised was lightly touched with mascara, face powder and lipstick so dark red it was damn near black. Her eyes were a dark, penetrating blue, long-lashed under bold black arching eyebrows.

Standing next to where she sat by a framed sketch of a nude woman, I asked, "Dr. Winters?"

Though of course I knew....

Her smile was lovely, emphasizing apple cheeks that were a wholesome surprise in that sophisticated mug of hers.

"Mr. Starr," she purred, extending her hand, which I took

and shook, a warm slender thing with long-nailed tapering fingers, "from now on, I'm going to call you 'Jack' and you're going to call me 'Sylvia.' "

"Fine." I grinned and sat. "I may even get around to calling you 'Syl,' if you let me."

Her smile turned amused and made her chin crinkle. "Let's not get ahead of ourselves. What can I do for you, Jack?"

"Well, I already got ahead of myself, didn't I? The first thing I should have done was thank you for meeting me."

"I was intrigued. But as I told you on the phone, I'm very limited as to what I can say about my patients."

"Patient privacy," I said with a nod. "Sure, I get that."

"I don't want to mislead you." She leaned in, as if about to share a secret. "I *am* a doctor, but not a medical one."

"Ah. Psychologist, not psychiatrist."

"Exactly." She leaned back. "Would you like something to drink?"

She was having coffee, not espresso, and like Maggie she took it heavily laced with cream.

"Yeah, please," I said, and she waved the waitress over.

I liked that. Sylvia Winters had a natural yet feminine strength, expressed in something as small but telling as being the one of us to call for service. Smart, beautiful, stacked, and if that sounds like I'm a rogue, let me remind you that I put "smart" first on that list.

The slender, not unattractive waitress in a black blouse and black skirt and black stockings (was she going for vampire or nun?) came over. When I asked for a Coca-Cola, she looked at me for a long time, the way a bartender in a western looks at a dude who orders sarsaparilla.

So I sneered at her and said, "In a dirty glass."

That made her laugh. You make one of these sullen girls laugh, you must have something. And Sylvia was smiling, too.

"You live here in the Village," I said.

"And work."

"I'm sure you have no shortage of patients."

One side of her mouth smiled; her lips were neither full nor thin, just well-defined, as if by an artist more adept than any showcasing their work on the walls of the Gateway.

"No shortage of patients," she admitted. "But they sometimes have a shortage of funds."

"How long have you been at it?"

"This is my third year, since graduating."

That made sense. I made her as maybe twenty-five, twenty-six.

"I'm not poverty-stricken, understand," she said. "I have a number of patients in entertainment and the arts. There are some talented and successful actors, artists and musicians who live in the Village. They like to soak up the atmosphere."

"I dig it down here, too. Notice I used the word 'dig.' Just to impress you with how hep I am. Or is that hip?"

She chuckled. "I admit I like the bohemian way of life around here. Little movie theaters with foreign films, Italian restaurants every second or third step, bars filled with writers and artists, every night a party, but an intellectually stimulating one."

"Has its attractions."

She shrugged, sipped her coffee. Her nails were painted the same red-black as her mouth. "There are a lot of pretenders, sure, and kids who are spending a few years learning if they can or can't make it in the arts."

"Or till their parents get tired of subsidizing them."

"Or till then. But who am I to judge? My living here *is* partly economic."

My Coke came, set in front of me with a clunk. No glass. Warm.

I thanked the waitress, who had gotten over finding me amusing, and she moved to a table across the room.

I said to Sylvia, "She's just jealous of you. So...economical to live in the Village, is it?"

"It's *cheap* to live in the Village." Again she leaned in to share a secret. "Would you believe? I have a big, beautiful, one-bedroom apartment on 11th Street and Seventh Avenue. One hundred a month."

Dr. Frederick's suite in the Waldorf Towers went for maybe ten times that, or more.

"Can't beat that kinda overhead," I said. "And you work out of there, too, right?"

"Yes. So. Jack. Have we sufficiently broken the ice? I'm already rather taken with you, and from your expression, I can see that you are already in love with me. By the time I'm through with my coffee, I expect a proposal of marriage."

I took a swig of Coke and grinned at her. "I *was* going to pop the question, till I heard you didn't have that lucrative a set-up. I mean, the psychiatrist or even psychologist *I* marry will have to have a really thriving practice. Keeping me in creature comforts is a commitment."

Her smile was again one-sided, devilish. "You kid on the square, don't you, Jack?"

I pretended to frown. "On the other hand, maybe I don't want to marry a shrink. But just to be clear?"

"Yes?"

"I am willing to fool around with one."

She almost did a spit take with her coffee, laughing. The waitress, sitting bored across the room from us, frowned, either really jealous or maybe just not wanting to be interrupted as she read the latest issue of *Craze*, which Bob Price would have loved.

"Now, for the record, I'm willing to buy you food," I said. "I hear the grub here is pretty good. It's a little early, but we're beating the crowd. What say?"

"Okay, okay," she said, holding up her hands in surrender, "consider the ice well and truly broken. As far as you buying me supper, we'll see. What is it I can do for you?"

"Well," I said, businesslike now, "as I mentioned on the phone, I want to discuss our mutual friend, Bob Price."

I'd told her that the Starr Syndicate was contemplating getting into business with Bob by way of a *Craze* comic strip.

"You're aware," I said, getting into an area we had *not* discussed in our brief phone conversation, "that Bob has volunteered to testify tomorrow in that Senate hearing."

"On juvenile delinquency and comic books, yes. He's quite adamant about that."

"I'm afraid he's going to get himself in trouble."

Her expression was placid, her eyes almost sleepy, but that was deceiving: the sharp intelligence in those eyes was examining me like a surgeon with a blade.

She said, "I understand he's written, or anyway is writing, an opening statement that he's quite proud of."

"I have no doubt it will be a masterpiece. But once he's given his golden spiel, he'll have to answer questions, and he won't be prepared for that. I promise you."

"He's a very intelligent man."

"And an excitable boy. I saw him shortly before I phoned you this afternoon, Sylvia. He's hopped up and strung out, as we hip Village types put it. My guess is he's popping Dexies like they were Lifesavers. And they're not. Life savers."

She nodded, but said nothing. Patient/doctor thing again.

I leaned forward, took advantage of the nice rapport we'd established. "Look. I'm not asking for you to reveal anything about Bob. Frankly, I think I already understand him perfectly. His father made him feel worthless, and now he's beating his dead dad at his own game, the funny-book business. Then this Doc Frederick comes along, playing disapproving Daddy again, not just where Bob's concerned but everybody in America, which Bob is resentful as hell about. Pissed-off is the psychological term, in case you skipped class that day."

Her chin lifted, and her eyes were no longer hooded. "That wasn't bad. Maybe you should take night school and join my profession."

"Maybe. I do some of my best work with a couch." I gave her half a smile and she gave me the other half.

"So you'd like me," she said, "to advise Mr. Price not to testify."

I flipped a hand. "He volunteered. He can back out the same way. He can give a statement to the press saying he did not feel he could get a fair hearing in that kind of witch-hunt atmosphere, and just walk."

She was thinking.

"Well?" I asked.

She sighed. "I agree with you. I know what lousy shape Bob is in. He didn't get those pills from me, by the way. I'm not a medical doctor, remember."

"I remember. So will you advise him to bail out?"

Her eyes, her smile, were unfathomably sad. "Jack, I have. I already have."

Shit.

"I was afraid of that," I said. This time *I* sighed. "He is strong-headed. Would you call him, and give it one last try?"

"Certainly. I'm happy to. But I don't hold out much hope. Was there…anything else?"

She just might have been fishing for a date—hey, I am pretty cute—but then I recalled Maggie's other agenda.

"Sylvia, I need to ask you about another patient of yours."

This time her smile wasn't at all amused. She folded her arms. "Really, Jack? Maybe I should hand my notes over to you on all of my patients."

"Just Will Allison."

Her head moved to one side, slightly, and she frowned in thought; the arc of platinum hair covered her face slightly. "Will?"

"Yeah. That kid really lost his head the other night at the Strip Joint. *The Barray Soiree*?"

Her expression softened but her eyes remained sharp. "Oh. Yes. I *saw* that."

"Listen, I've been around violence. I was an MP during the war. I thought there was edge in that kid's attitude. I had the weird feeling, if he hadn't been camera-shy, he might have slugged that Lehman character, and maybe Barray, too."

"…What do you want to know?"

"*Would* he do something violent like that? *Could* he?

More generally, does the boy have mental problems that make him a bad risk for us?"

Her eyes narrowed. "You're thinking of taking him on as a cartoonist for Starr?"

"Very preliminary thinking, but yeah. What do you say?"

"I really *can't* say, Jack."

I winked at her. "Which translates as, the kid's screwed up. A bad risk."

"I didn't say that!" She touched her forehead. "Jack, completely off the record...nothing you can hold me to...I will tell you I think Will's just a young, insecure kid, messed up but no worse, or more dangerous, than any other typical young guy starting out in a tough field. You can report that to Maggie Starr, but I won't put it in writing."

"Fair enough," I said.

But something she'd said nudged me: *I won't put it in writing.*

"Listen, what's your opinion of Dr. Werner Frederick? He isn't your patient. *That* you can tell me."

Still, she thought for a moment. The waitress came over and refilled Sylvia's coffee. The girl asked me indifferently if I wanted another Coke and I said I didn't. I asked her how she liked that *Craze* comic book she was reading and she said it was okay. But she quickly returned to it like a seminary student reading "The Song of Solomon."

That had given Sylvia enough time to think, and she said, very evenly, "I am not a fan of Dr. Frederick's work on juvenile delinquency as it relates to comic books."

"Why?"

"I'd rather not say anything negative about a man who I otherwise admire. He spends much of his time working with underprivileged children, and his examination of the effects of segregation upon Negro youth is brave work, important work."

"Have you ever met him?"

"No. I would like to. I might enjoy arguing the case *for* comic books in child development."

"Well, I'd like to ask you to table that particular discussion."

"Why?"

"Because you might be working with Dr. Frederick."

She straightened and her smile was unguardedly enthusiastic. "Really? How is that, Jack?"

"Well, I'll tell you, Syl—right after I take you out for supper. How does El Chico sound?"

It sounded fine. But it wasn't until much later when we'd necked on her couch in her hundred-buck apartment for maybe half an hour that I sprung the idea on her of ghosting the doc's advice column.

I said I did some of my best work on couches.

CHAPTER FOUR

The morning was overcast and cold, not terrible weather but hardly the best spring might offer Manhattan. I'd left the top up on my snazzy little white Kaiser-Darrin when I escorted Bob Price to the federal courthouse at Foley Square. At the Entertaining Funnies office on Lafayette Street, his partner Hal Feldman declined to come along.

"I've tried to talk him out of testifying," Feldman had said. He looked like a cop who'd been trying for hours to talk a jumper in off a ledge. "He won't hear it."

"I know," I said. "I tried, Maggie tried, even his shrink tried."

"Stubborn jackass," he said, his Brooklyn-tinged baritone ragged. "Well, I can't watch it. I don't go to public executions. Somebody oughta shoot that damn Dr. Frederick."

Normally Hal was a dapper guy, but this morning his tailored blue suit seemed rumpled, his John Garfield-ish mug hadn't seen a razor yet, and his wavy dark hair was like a squirmy nest of black snakes. In his mid-twenties, Feldman clearly had been sitting up all night. With a sick friend, as it turned out.

He sighed, grinned wearily, clasped my shoulder. "I'm just glad Bob's got you to babysit him now, Jack."

"Happy to, Hal. Just so everybody understands I don't change diapers." I checked my watch. "We ought to head out."

The editor shook his head. "He's still working on that god-damn opening statement."

I frowned. "Hell, I thought sure he'd be finished by *now*. Hasn't he been working on it for days?"

"More like weeks." Feldman lighted up a Camel. His eyes were bloodshot. "All night, he's been alternating NoDoz and that diet medication of his."

"Dexedrine, you mean?"

Feldman nodded wearily. "He's *eager* to go down there, Jack, into that lions' den, can you buy it? Thinks he's doing the *right* thing, the *noble* thing. Says he's a friendly witness, and certainly these senators, as good patriotic Americans, will wanna do what's right, too. You know, listen to reason."

"That isn't the way things work in real life."

"Jesus," Feldman said, rolling his eyes, "that ain't even the way it works in our *comic* books."

Not surprisingly, I'd found Bob Price at his desk, typing away, wadded balls of discarded typewriter paper over-flowing his trash can, cigarette stubs overflowing his ashtray, desktop littered with empty paper coffee cups.

"Time, Bob," I said.

Fingers flying at the typewriter keys, he said, "Just a second. Just a second."

I dragged him out of his office and into the waiting arms of the unshaven Feldman, who had gotten his partner in front of a mirror with an electric razor, and helped him into a clean suit. Price was like a prospective groom who'd tied one on the night before, and had to be pieced and patched together for the big ceremony.

Which made me the ring bearer, I guess.

At least we weren't late. In fact, we were fifteen minutes early, and we had to move through a group of reporters, their cameras and notepads at the ready, before we could get past the Grecian columns that flanked the entry. Somehow Harry Barray had wrangled a press pass, though if the big blond disc jockey with the puffy features was a reporter, I was J. Edgar Hoover.

But Barray was the only member of the press contingent who recognized the comic book publisher, or at least the only one who accosted Price with any pre-hearing questions, shoving a microphone in his face and saying, "Good morning, Bob. Are you anticipating any trouble inside?"

In Barray's defense, this was hardly a hostile question, but Price snapped at him like a bulldog on a short leash.

"Any trouble I get is the fault of people like you," Price said, eyes bulging, spittle flying, "who trample the rights of good Americans to read and write what they please! Comic book readers are citizens, too, you know!"

Barray backed away, looking damn near scared. I could hardly blame him.

Inside the courthouse, where footsteps echoed like one gunshot after another, Price grinned at me, his eyes glittering behind his round-lensed dark-framed glasses.

"See, Jack? I set that character straight, didn't I? Show guys like that the error of their ways, and they'll come around. They *will* come around."

"Are you kidding?" I said. "You scared the shit out of Barray. He'll tell his listeners you behaved like a maniac."

He blinked, eyes owlish behind the lenses. "Why would he do that?"

I ignored that absurdity and instead said, "You still have time to head out a side door. I'll go in and say you were too sick to testify."

His cheeks reddened—he might have been blushing, but he wasn't. "Goddamnit, Jack, I *want* to testify! This is my big chance!"

"Well, ease off. Stay calm and don't look and act like a monster that jumped out of one of your funny books."

That threw him, even hurt him a little, but he said nothing, and I escorted him by the arm into Room 110, where the Kefauver crime hearings had first been held, till the public interest sent them into larger quarters upstairs.

We found our way into the good-sized chamber where burnished oak rode the walls and floors and even the furniture. Reserved seats awaited us at the front of the ten-row spectator section at left. At a long central bench four congressmen (including Senator Estes Kefauver himself) were taking their seats. The room was cool and they left their suit coats on as they settled in.

Near their bench was an astonishing display that disrupted the courtroom's austerity in an explosion of garish colors and grotesque images. On easels were two dozen blow-ups of full-color comic-book covers: *Tales from the Vault*, *Fighting Crime*, *Weird Fantastic Science*, *Suspense Crime Stories*, *Weird Terror*, *True Criminals*, *Beware!*, and more. Starring in these poster-size exhibits were walking corpses, machine-gunning gangsters, rampaging werewolves, drooling space creatures, and leggy gun molls showing off their .38 revolvers and heaving "headlights."

Possibly also 38s, come to think of it.

I pointed out this display to Price.

"You're screwed," I whispered.

He glanced at the array of covers—potentially the most damaging witnesses of all, and most of them EF publications—and shrugged as if to say, "So what?"

The witness table sat before the bench but at a forty-five degree angle, so that the spectators could also view the testimony. The witness chair was angled to prevent eye contact between those testifying and those questioning (and, for that matter, those observing). A trio of stenographers were positioned nearby, one man, two women.

On both the witness table and bench were arrays of microphones with a nest of heavy cables on the floor, snaking behind the spectator seating, where (up on a platform) TV and newsreel men, their cameras as big as robots in a science-fiction film, were waiting for the fun to begin. As the seats around and behind us quickly filled in, I was reminded of the bustling tension you encountered on a movie set.

Senator Kefauver was the draw here—his crime hearings had been a big hit on TV, making a star out of him (and the sweating, twitching manicured hands of camera-shy witness, gangster Frank Calabria). But the man in charge was New Jersey Senator Robert C. Hendrickson.

So it was Chairman Hendrickson who, at 10 A.M., spoke into the microphone and called the proceedings to order. He was a straight-laced type, mustached, bespectacled and in his mid-fifties, his thinning, silver hair combed slickly back on a bucket head. He had the humorless demeanor of a high school principal in a Henry Aldrich movie.

"Today and tomorrow," he began lugubriously, "the United States Subcommittee on Investigating Juvenile Delinquency is going into the problem of comic books…"

So, they'd already decided it was a problem.

"...illustrating stories depicting crime or dealing with horror and sadism."

To be fair, the committee chairman did claim that their work was not as a board of censorship.

"We want to determine what damage, if any," Hendrickson declared, "is being done to our children's minds by certain types of publications."

First up was not a witness, but a slide show of comic-book panels that alternately depicted scenes of blood-spattered horror or bullet-spraying crime, with occasional "head-lights" panels tossed in. Some images were genuinely dis-turbing, as when a hypo wielded by a madman seemed poised to plunge into the wide-open eye of a lovely young woman. This stuff made the array of violent covers on those looming easels look like kid's stuff.

Which of course was the problem—the assumption by these stuffed shirts that only little kids read these comic books. Hell, the EF line was clearly for teenagers and adults. Despite the vivid, detailed horrors of the artwork, you couldn't tell what was going on if you didn't read the cap-tions and speech balloons. Feldman was a guy who seemed to be getting paid by the word.

No kid under eleven would be able to read this copy-heavy stuff, much less understand it. And those older kids who could read it needed to be smart. You know—literate.

But that wasn't touched on, not at all. Committee execu-tive director Richard Clendenen—lean, middle-aged, with a square jaw right out of an Americana superhero comic book —narrated the slide show with unctuous pre-judgement: "Typically, these comic books portray almost all kinds of crime, committed through extremely cruel, sadistic and punitive acts."

At several points, Clendenen singled out particularly violent, disturbing panels as prime examples of the content of comic books published by Entertaining Funnies.

"I mention this," Clendenen said, "because the publisher of that firm will be appearing before this committee later this morning."

The implication was that Price had been summoned, when of course he had volunteered.

Following the slide presentation, various documents were introduced as exhibits from assorted government agencies, as well as newspaper and magazine articles criticizing comic books and linking them to juvenile delinquency—the majority written by one Dr. Werner Frederick.

Then the first witness was called, a mental health expert with New York's so-called "Family Court." Surprisingly, he did not join in on the anti-comics theme. Some of his colleagues (he said) considered certain comic books potentially worthy of "stronger criticism," while others found them essentially harmless.

The second witness was a representative of a comic-book association of publishers, printers and distributors that had attempted, without any particular success, to provide the comics business with a self-monitoring group like Hollywood's Breen Office. This testimony was long-winded and flip-flopped between pandering to the panel, and defending comics as "a great medium."

But it managed to go on long enough that Bob Price— scheduled for the morning—got bumped to the afternoon. I hauled him off to a deli for lunch, and he had a sandwich and a Coke, just like me. But I passed on dessert—Price's choice, more Dexies and NoDoz, killed what was left of my appetite.

"You should lay off that stuff," I said.

"If I do, I'll fall asleep up there."

"How long has it been, Bob, since you had a decent night's sleep?"

"…What day is it?"

The sky was almost black as we walked back. Price didn't seem to notice. He was smiling. He had bounce in his step.

"I can't wait to get up there," he said, raising victory fists to his paunch.

"Just stay cool," I said.

"You bet, boy. You bet."

But his eyes were as wild as a zombie's on an EF cover.

After lunch, however, Price was not (as we both had expected) the first witness up.

Dr. Werner Frederick was.

With his background as a forensic psychiatrist for the city, the doc was an old hand at testifying—he knew it was theater, and had dressed for the occasion: a white jacket over a white shirt with a simple black necktie. As if he'd just arrived from the lab, where he'd found a cure for cancer or, better yet, comic books.

He even turned his chair to the right, a little, so he could face the committee.

Initially he was asked to describe his new book *Ravage the Lambs*, a softball question if ever there was one. He replied by detailing the work with troubled children and adolescents that had gone into this "sober, painstaking, laborious clinical study."

The S.O.B. was writing his own cover blurbs!

Despite that thick German accent, his tone was clear and piercing, his voice ringing in the room, and he'd have made a great B-movie scientist, particularly a mad one.

When he really wanted to make a point, he slowed things way down, phrasing for effect.

"It is my opinion," he said, "without any reasonable doubt …and without any reservation…that comic books…are an important…*contributing*…factor…in *many* cases…of juvenile delinquency."

"I've never seen this guy in person before," Price whispered to me. His right leg was shaking. "Look at him! He's so goddamn *smug*…and *sarcastic.*"

"Don't you be," I advised.

The committee let Frederick rail on and on. When asked what kind of child was most likely to be affected by crime comic books, he claimed, "Primarily the normal child. The most morbid children are less affected by comic books because they are wrapped up in their own fantasies."

He was good, he was eloquent, but he was also German, and while the U.S. government loved German scientists, the American public didn't. That much Price had going for him.

Ironically, prejudice of another sort was what Frederick got into next. He spoke of an EF story that used the word "Spick" and promoted (Frederick claimed) bigotry.

"I think Hitler is a beginner compared to the comic-book industry," Frederick said. "They get the children much younger, teach them race hatred at the age of four, before they could read."

From the spectator seats behind us, a voice cried out, *"You're a liar! You are a goddamn* menace!"

Will Allison again.

I hadn't seen him come in, yet there he was, not in J.D. drag this time, rather a suit and tie, like a kid heading to prom. But his eyes, his hair, his expression, were those of a wild man.

Hendrickson rapped his gavel. "*Guards!* Escort that man out!"

Allison continued to shout his protests as a pair of uniformed guards yanked him bodily from the audience and hauled him struggling out of the chamber.

Price didn't have to whisper, because a general murmur of excitement filled the courtroom as he informed me, "Will illustrated the story that creep said was bigoted. It's an *anti*-bigotry story, Jack. That bastard Frederick *has* to know that!"

"And misrepresented it, to take a cheap shot."

"Damn right." Price's eyes were tight behind the glasses, and he was shaking that big oblong head. "Well, that's it— I'm gonna *get* that bastard."

And Price soon got his chance: he was the next up to testify. Once again, Dr. Frederick had warmed up a chair for him. In his loose-fitting, rather bulky pale gray suit, Price looked even heavier than he was, and he was already sweating. He brought a briefcase to the witness table, removed his prepared speech and other notes, and took his seat.

"Gentleman," Price said, "I would like to make a short statement."

This was allowed, and the comic book publisher gave his name and outlined his credentials, including his certification to teach in New York City public high schools. He reminded them that he was there as a voluntary witness.

What followed was an admirably well-written, if haltingly delivered history of his father's beginnings in "the comic magazine" field, a business which Leo Price had "virtually created," in so doing fostering an industry that employed thousands and gave entertainment to millions. He moved on to his own involvement, after his father's passing, which included continuing to publish his father's beloved Bible stories comics.

(This was something of a white lie: Leo had printed way too many copies of his Bible comics, and all son Bob did was fill from the warehouse the occasional Sunday school orders that came in for them.)

Then Price opened the door: "I also publish horror comics. I was the first publisher in these United States to publish horror comics. I am responsible. I started them. Some may not like them, but that's a matter of personal taste."

The boldness of that was appealing. In fact, the whole statement was fine, just swell, only he was just reading it, never looking up, occasionally stumbling over his own words, pausing to dab the sweat from his brow with a hanky, and that leg of his was shaking again. More violently now.

"My father," he said, "was proud of the comics he published. I am proud of the comics *I* publish. We use the best writers, the finest artists, and spare nothing to make each magazine, each story, each page a work of art."

Maybe it was a good thing Price was looking down at those typewritten pages: he was spared the skeptical expressions the senators at the bench exchanged, some glancing back at the looming grotesque comic-book cover blow-ups.

"Reading for entertainment has never harmed anyone,"

Price was saying. "Our American children are for the most part normal and bright. But those adults who would prohibit comic magazines see our kids as dirty, sneaky, perverted monsters who use the comics as a blueprint for action. Are we afraid of our own children? Are they so evil, so simple-minded, that all it takes is a story of murder to convince them to murder? A story of robbery to inspire them to robbery?"

Finally, he set down his papers and began to speak from his head and his heart—perhaps not a wise move, but even as well-crafted as his prepared statement was, I was pleased to see him stop reading and just talk to the panel.

"I need to point out that when Dr. Frederick spoke of one of our magazines preaching racial intolerance, he was indulging in an outrageous half-truth. Yes, the word 'Spick' appears in it. But the doctor neglected to tell you what the plot of the story was—that it was one of a series of stories designed to show the evils of race prejudice and mob violence, in this case against Mexican Catholics. Previous stories have dealt with anti-Semitism, anti-Negro feelings, as well as the evils of dope addiction and the development of juvenile delinquents. And I am very proud of that."

A good off-the-cuff response, I thought, but it soon degenerated into a back-and-forth between Price and the committee's junior counsel over the inconsistency of the publisher claiming comics were merely entertainment that made no impact upon young readers, when these social-comment tales were obviously designed to make just such an impact.

This seemed to rattle Price, who—caught in a defensible

inconsistency—just couldn't handle himself under questioning. He might have, and probably could have, if he hadn't been fading.

But fading he was.

That Dexie high of his was descending into its inevitable limp-rag aftermath. He just sat there getting pummeled, like a punch-drunk boxer, head down, sweat drops flying, just taking it. At least his leg wasn't shaking anymore.

Then star performer Kefauver got into the act. The senator was a lanky road company Lincoln with sharp eyes behind tortoise-shell glasses. He was not wearing his famous coonskin hat, if you're wondering.

"Mr. Price, let me get the limits as far as what you will put in one of your magazines." He had a cornpone drawl that you mistook for easygoing at your own peril.

"Certainly," Price said.

"Do you think a child can be hurt by something he reads or sees?"

"I don't believe so, no."

"Is the sole test of what you publish, then, based on whether or not it sells? Is there any *limit* to your, ah, entertainment?"

Price's chin was up, but his eyes looked tired. "My only limits are the bounds of good taste. What I consider good taste."

"Your own good taste, then, and the sales potential of your product?"

"Yes."

Kefauver held up a copy of a *Suspense Crime Stories* comic book whose cover depicted a terrified woman in mid-air, having fallen from a window where the silhouetted hands of her assailant could still be seen in push mode. The woman was screaming, staring wide-eyed at us as she looked through us at the oncoming (off-camera) pavement. Terror-struck, screaming or not, she was very attractive, in a skimpy night-gown, that showed off her shapely legs and, of course, her…headlights.

"Do you think *this* is in good taste, Mr. Price?"

"Yes, sir, I do, for the cover of a crime comic."

"What might constitute *bad* taste here?"

"Well, we could have depicted her *after* she'd fallen."

"You mean her body on the pavement?"

"Yes."

"And that would be worse?"

"Yes. Showing her twisted corpse, blood everywhere, bones sticking out of her shattered limbs, that would be a cover in bad taste."

Kefauver's drawl was so folksy, it was like Tennessee Ernie Ford giving you the third degree. "And you decided against that. In a display of eminent good taste, your artist depicted a scantily clad female screaming in terror as she falls from a great height, with her life about to end?"

"Yes."

Bob Price saw nothing wrong. And the reporters and the cameras saw him seeing that.

Me, I just sat there watching the spectacle of a guy falling from a great height without even screaming. Without even a shove.

He was a shambling wreck when, an hour later, they had finally finished wringing out every ounce of humiliation from him ("So this decapitated head held by a man also holding a bloody axe, that would be in bad taste if you showed *more* blood?"), and sent him along on what they clearly considered to be his vile business. His loose-fitting suit was soaked with sweat now, the flesh on his face hanging like a balloon that had lost maybe a third of its air. He had done everything wrong, stopping short only of rolling ball bearings in his fingers like Captain Queeg.

The reporters were on us like kids swarming Martin and Lewis, only this bunch didn't want a signed picture. They were yelling questions.

"Hey Bob! Do you really think horror comics are in 'good taste'?"

"Bob, over here! How much blood is okay for a comic cover?"

"What will you do if Congress bans horror comics?"

I was escorting him through the crowd, grateful that he wasn't answering any of the questions, keeping his head down. At least he didn't cover his face like a criminal, though clearly that's how he was being treated by the press boys.

But then that was how he'd been treated by those patriotic Congressmen as well, hadn't he?

Suddenly—and whether planned or accidental, I couldn't tell you—we were facing Dr. Werner Frederick, pristine in his white jacket, like he'd arrived to haul Price and me off to the loony bin. He'd stepped out from behind a pillar like that doctor who shot Huey Long.

"Mr. Price," Frederick said with nasty pleasantness, "I just want to tell you in person that I find reprehensible what you're doing to today's youth."

The sight of the doctor and the sound of his German-inflected condemnation broke through the torpor of the Dexie crash, and Bob Price came alive. It was as if that other doctor, Frankenstein, had thrown a switch and sent electricity pulsing through the publisher's dead flesh, reanimating it.

"You *lied*, you son of a bitch," Price spat at him.

"I would *expect* that kind of language from a peddler of filth," the psychiatrist said, sneering.

"You bastard…"

I was tugging Price along, but he was fighting me.

Frederick, raising his voice, reporters circling like the vultures they were, said, "My book *Ravage the Lambs* is about to appear, gentlemen, and perhaps you aren't aware that it's been chosen as a Book of the Month Club selection."

Price snarled, "You used artwork from *my* comics without permission! I'm going to sue you. I'll get an *injunction*!"

"Gentlemen," Frederick said to the reporters, "you are my witnesses! This is the sinister hand of a corrupter of children threatening to prevent the distribution of my book… because it exposes him as the father of juvenile delinquents across our great nation."

Price was doing his best to squirm out of my grasp. "I'll *kill* you, you bastard! I'll *kill* you, so help me God!"

But before Price could strangle the smirking shrink in front of dozens of witnesses, I regained my purchase on his arm and dragged him through the crowd and outside. His energy was soon drained and when I got him into the convertible, he quickly fell asleep.

Not a restful sleep on our drive back to Lafayette Street, no. Filled with nightmares.

Monsters, no doubt. With German accents and white lab coats.

CHAPTER FIVE

Early evening and it seemed like everybody and his dog was on the street in Harlem, from "high-yaller" whore to good church-going lady, from bow-tie businessman to toothless derelict. Raucous music bled from bars and clubs, and the smell of fried food wafted. Laughter, high and hearty, cut across traffic sounds, but so did angry yells. This was that big multi-colored neon-washed canvas called Harlem—110th, 116th, 125th, and 135th Streets, Seventh Avenue, Lenox Avenue, the west side of Fifth Avenue from 110th up—bustling, pulsing, threatening, vulgar, poetic.

Time was when a downtown "ofay" like me came up here to dig the jazz at Birdland or maybe dance at the Savoy. That was back when side-street after-hours joints flourished by ignoring New York's candy-ass legal closing time of four A.M. If I were so inclined, I could tell you of wild nights that ended with me and a date stumbling out of a smoke-filled basement hideaway into unforgiving sunlight.

No more.

In this small section of the city, a population of 700,000, largely colored, made up what one Broadway columnist called "a concentration camp surrounded by the barbed-wire fence of ironclad prejudice." Scant new housing had been built here in decades, and the deteriorating firetraps where so many lived in squalor and discomfort were largely owned by white millionaires to whom the notion of improving sanitation was almost as funny as the high rents they squeezed out of their piss-poor tenants.

Those who could afford to had long since moved to the Sugar Hill area, or to one of the quiet, respectable tree-shaded streets away from Harlem's business district, if by business you mean robbery, murder, rape, mugging, prostitution and dope-peddling.

Not that there weren't respectable merchants and other businesses in Harlem. But the cops shrugged off complaints, and cast a blind eye toward misdemeanors and felonies they personally witnessed. And the newspapers rarely bothered publishing anything about Harlem crime, spiking most items with that address.

A fair share of all that ignored criminal activity was perpetrated by teen gangs, like the Sabers, the Barons, the Chancellors, among others. Such gangs often fought each other for the sheer hell of it—those "rumbles" you've heard about—but their life's blood was robbery, whether purse-snatching or armed hold-ups.

These gangs offered protection, a sense of belonging, walking around money, and in-house "debs," girls of twelve and up, who kept the boys happy. The temptation for a Harlem youth to join, not to mention the peer pressure, was as overwhelming as Harlem itself.

That's what Dr. Frederick was up against with his free clinic for troubled kids, operating out of St. Phillip's Episcopal Church of Harlem.

"As much as I might disagree with his attack on comic books," Sylvia Winters told me, from the rider's seat of my convertible, "I admire his overall effort to bring mental health care to the underprivileged."

I had picked Sylvia up at her apartment and we had plenty of time to talk on the way, between traffic and the scores of blocks between the Village and St. Phillip's.

The overcast day never paid off with rain, but the evening remained cool, so I kept the top up. Anyway, you have to shout in a top-down convertible, to hold a decent conversation, and I wanted to explore Sylvia's feelings and opinions about Dr. Frederick before we signed her up to ghost his column.

"Well," I said, "the doc specifically wanted to meet you up at his free clinic. I'm not sure why."

"I think I know," she said.

"Why so?"

She was in another of her bulky sweater and slacks combos, this one a dark blue that hit her eye color dead bang. That platinum hair of hers, in that shortish cut, showed no roots at all. I wondered if she was naturally platinum blonde. I wondered if I'd find out....

"Couple of things," she said. "Dr. Frederick probably wants to make sure I'm comfortable coming to see him in Harlem—it's not the friendliest area to a young white woman, you know."

"Actually," I said, "it can be way *too* friendly."

She nodded with a humorless half-smile. "If the doctor and I are working together, I may have to come up there from time to time. He also may hope to enlist me as a part-time volunteer—none of his staff is paid, I understand, and I have a degree, after all."

"Is that everything?"

She shook her head. "He may be showing off a little. Letting me know Dr. Werner Frederick is more than just a pop psychiatrist who likes to get in the papers and magazines and on TV and radio."

I grunted a laugh. "That he's a real, dedicated professional."

Her expression was thoughtful. "And I think he is. But when he was working as a forensic psychiatrist for the New York courts, he came in contact with a bunch of juvenile offenders, who liked to read comic books."

"Imagine that."

"He took a look at some of the more violent comic books, and all that blood on pulp paper was like blood in the water to him."

"How so?"

"He smelled a subject, a controversy, all his own. And that's another reason for him to establish his credibility with me."

"Yeah?"

And another nod. "He knows a good number of mental-health care professionals think he's as full of crap as a Christmas goose, where funny books are concerned. That his thinking is simplistic, and that his research is…I don't know how else to say this, Jack…shoddy."

"How is it shitty?"

"I said 'shoddy.' "

That had made her smile, but now she hesitated, obviously reluctant to criticize a fellow "mental-health care professional."

Finally she admitted, "The man has no real data. Just an

opinion that comic books in general—which something like ninety percent of children read these days—set a bad example. In Dr. Frederick's view, there is violence in comic books, and a lot of so-called juvenile delinquents read comic books, therefore comic books cause juvenile delinquency."

We were at a light in midtown. "Isn't that one of those false syllogisms they taught me about in college, right before I flunked out?"

Her half-smile was better than a full smile from most females. "Very good, Jack. No, the doctor is just riding the comet of a controversy of his own creation. He *has* no proof."

"You wouldn't have thought so at that Senate hearing this afternoon."

She shrugged. "It's because the senators, like Dr. Frederick, begin with an anti-comic-book assumption as false as that syllogism. It's simply bad science."

"Isn't that a comic book Entertaining Funnies publishes —*Bad Science*?"

We were moving again.

She leaned back in her comfy, pleated vinyl bucket seat. "Anyway, everything Dr. Frederick says about comic books is based on undocumented anecdotes."

"But he claims *Ravage the Lambs* is chock full of data."

"Sure. Such as, if he runs across a comic book with a gory scene of suicide by hanging, he lines it up with a juvenile suicide in his files. Or if a child or adolescent commits a robbery or assault or even a murder, he finds a similar crime in a comic book."

"A comic book that was a favorite of these bad seeds?"

She shook her head again. "No. Frederick doesn't bother

making that connection, probably because he can't. Beyond that 'data,' it's just opinion—Wonder Guy uses force to subdue a gangster, Dr. Frederick sees fascism."

I grinned at her. "And if Batwing lives with his young ward Sparrow, it's obviously a homosexual relationship."

"Not to mention pedophilia."

"I try not." I honked at a double-parked cab. Guess what good it did. "Then why are you willing to ghost his column for us?"

She was staring out into the geometric abstraction of New York City at night. "Because I think his heart is in the right place, and—beyond this dead comic-book horse he's flogging—a lot of what he's done, and *is* doing, is enormously positive."

"And that's the only reason?"

She smiled at me, vaguely teasing. "Well…maybe I want to work with the Starr Syndicate so I have an excuse to see you, Jack."

I gave her a leer that wasn't vague at all. "Or maybe you like the sound of that twenty grand Maggie promised you, if Doc Frederick approves of you."

"Maybe," she admitted, with a knowing smirk.

Man, this chickie was as smart as she was beautiful, and I was just enough of a free-thinking man not to hold that against her. Maybe I should marry her. After all, having an in-house shrink might help keep a guy sane, and the extra income would be no hardship. See? Free-thinking.

St. Philip's Episcopal was a massive brown-brick neo-Gothic affair at West 134th Street, just west of Seventh Avenue, well-known as the biggest church in Harlem with some two thousand members, including Adam Clayton Powell. I left the

Kaiser-Darrin locked up tight in the parking lot behind the big church, glad to have it off the street, but went in the front way, where the pastor's secretary pointed us to the nearby parish house whose basement was home to the clinic.

After the toweringly impressive church, the crumbling brownstone parish house came as a shock. Sole access was down a dingy, garbage-strewn alley. Should I have brought my gun?

After all these years, I thought, *back in a Harlem basement hideaway....*

A white sign bore the black-lettered words LAFARGUE CLINIC — WATCH YOUR STEP, which might have been psychiatric advice or maybe it meant the crumbled-stairs walkdown to a door that was unlocked. I wondered how many winos and armed robbers wandered in here unannounced.

A colored gent in his thirties greeted us; he wore a lab coat like the one Frederick had worn at the hearing today, and a big smile.

"You must be Dr. Winters," he said. He was mustached and wore glasses and if he'd been any more likable, I'd have bust out crying. "And you must be Mr. Starr. I'm Dr. Tweed."

We shook hands, and exchanged a few pleasantries. He'd been expecting us, and seemed particularly pleased to be meeting Sylvia, whether because she was a knockout or a fellow shrink, I couldn't tell you.

"We only have these two rooms," he said in a resonant baritone, gesturing around him. "We do our best to keep the moisture out, but it's a losing battle."

Never mind keeping the moisture out—how about the rats?

But they'd done their best to transform the uninviting

space into something pleasant, painting the cement walls white, doing the same with the open wooden rafters, putting down some linoleum. The larger of the two rooms had various play areas for younger children, tables, chairs, toys—blocks, pick-up sticks and dolls for the younger ones, Mr. Potato Head, sliding number puzzles and Matchbox cars for the older ones. Reading material was scattered around, Little Golden Books, *Highlights* magazine, but no comic books, not on your life, not even a *Donald* damn *Duck*.

Half a dozen men and women in lab coats supervised—several Negroes, mostly white folks—kneeling to talk to individual children, strictly colored. In one corner, half a dozen teens sat talking with a white shrink, in what appeared to be an informal group session. The smaller room down at the end of the space was for private conferences.

Dr. Frederick was in one of those now.

"So this is a free clinic?" I asked, really just making conversation.

"Essentially," Dr. Tweed said. "We charge twenty-five cents, unless a patient doesn't have it, in which case we are a free clinic. We charge fifty cents if we need to make a court appearance."

"Nobody's getting rich from rates like that."

"We only charge what we do to give our patients, usually their parents, a sense of worth. It goes for coffee, juice, snacks, for the kids and the staff."

Sylvia, hands fig-leafed before her, asked, "How often are you open?"

"Two evenings a week. It's all volunteer—we're up to eleven staffers now." He cast her a big smile. "But we could always use one *more*, Dr. Winters."

She returned the smile. "It does look like you're doing good work here."

"You know, Dr. Frederick is a great man. Most white psychiatrists won't even take on a Negro patient, let alone run a whole clinic for them."

"I have three Negro patients," Sylvia said, casually, not bragging. "But then I'm in the Village—most of my practice is people in the arts."

Dr. Frederick emerged from the smaller, glassed-in private-session room, holding the door open for a girl of about twelve. She, like the other kids, was dressed in nice if not fancy clothing, faded but not threadbare. School clothes.

I'll say one thing for Dr. Frederick—in that white lab coat, he looked like a goddamn doctor. Like the ones on TV who pitched toothpaste or spoke of the health benefits of smoking filter cigarettes. Moving with quick assurance, he came over and greeted us, shaking hands with Sylvia but only granting me a perfunctory nod.

"I've been checking up on you," Frederick said to her. It had a little unintended menace in it, thanks to that Eric von Stroheim accent of his.

"Nothing too damaging's turned up, I hope," she said, smiling but not overdoing.

"You've published some interesting papers," he said, "so obviously have you have writing skills. Your colleagues, your professors, say good things."

"You've been busy, Doctor." She seemed a little taken aback. "I thought you were testifying today."

"I have my researchers. You are an impressive young woman." The eyes behind the glasses were big as he said that, again imparting an unintentional menace—he meant her credentials, but from that expression on his narrow mug, he might have meant her…credentials.

"I would be honored to work with you," she said.

He raised a gently lecturing forefinger. "The emphasis will be on children, you understand. Advice to parents with so-called 'problem' children. That, of course, is not the nature of your practice."

"No," she admitted, "but I studied heavily in that field. My degree qualifies me to be a child psychologist, which is an area I hope to go into eventually."

That clearly pleased him. "Good. Good."

She risked a smile. "You know, my practice is in the Village, and most of the 'children' there are over twenty-one."

That got a chuckle out of him. "Has Dr. Tweed given you the tour? I'm afraid it's not the largest or best-appointed mental health clinic in New York."

"He has," she said, nodding toward Tweed, who was back working with some younger children. "Doctor, not meaning to sound obsequious, I do want you to know I admire your work here, and your work in general helping troubled young Negroes."

"Why, thank you, Dr. Winters."

The doc flicked a glance my way; he was irritated with me. I figured I knew why.

He was saying to her, "You understand that the topic of comic books will be off-limits in the column."

"Yes."

"That has to do with a conflict of interest we might have with the Starr Syndicate, which has ties to the so-called comic-book industry."

"Yes, I understand that limitation."

She didn't use this opening to mention her disagreement with his comic book theories, but I couldn't blame her. You don't go to the Twinkie factory for a job interview and mention that sugar rots the teeth.

"And you, young Mr. Starr," he said, turning a rather nasty smile on me. The place was lighted with florescent tubes that gave his pale pallor a ghostly glow.

"What about me?" I said pleasantly.

"We didn't have a chance to speak this afternoon. How is it that you were accompanying Mr. Price to the Senate hearing?"

Told you. I knew this was coming.

"His father and my father were friends and business partners," I said. "I've known Bob for years."

"Really? Mr. Price is enough of a friend for you to accompany him to Foley Square?"

I shrugged. "Bob's been getting death threats, for some reason, and he was also concerned about getting swamped by unfriendly press. I guess you know that wasn't just paranoia on his part...if you'll forgive the layman's use of the term."

His upper lip curled in that ghastly smile. "Well, Mr. Price is lucky to have such a good friend."

This didn't sound quite like sarcasm. Not quite.

"Well, there's a business connection, too," I said. "You should know, Doctor, before you sign with Starr Syndicate, that we are contemplating doing business with Mr. Price."

Maggie and I had discussed this. We felt full disclosure was both wise and ethical. We didn't need the doc to feel he'd been snookered, even if on some level we were in fact snookering him.

"What sort of business?" he asked, too casually, folding his arms.

"He publishes a humor comic book called *Craze*. You may be familiar with it."

He nodded. "In execrable taste, but likely the least offensive of his publications."

"Well, it's very popular. We're considering syndicating a Sunday page version of it—a comic strip spoofing other comic strips."

He thought about that. Here's what he had to be thinking: *Should he walk indignantly away from the Starr Syndicate offer, like an idiot, or should he pick up a big paycheck for lending his name to a column that the lovely Dr. Winters would largely write?*

Turned out he wasn't an idiot.

He said, "Business is business. I contemplated our arrangement with my eyes open, well understanding that the Starr Syndicate distributes comic strips. And I have no axe to grind where newspaper strips are concerned, for reasons you and your stepmother and I discussed."

And now, very belatedly, he offered his hand and I shook it.

"Do you mind my asking, Dr. Frederick," I said, "whether you did most of your research on *Ravage the Lambs* here at this clinic?"

His gesture around him was oddly dismissive. "We didn't set up shop here to research—we are providing our patients with psychiatric care. But of course in the process of that we *do* do research, just the same."

Sylvia probably thought I was baiting the guy, but I was really curious when I asked, "Did you find comic books contributed to any bad behavior with the kids you dealt with here?"

He nodded three or four times, emphatically. "Oh yes. For example, I had a twelve-year-old boy here tell me he admired 'tough guys.' I asked him, what's a tough guy? And he replied, 'A tough guy is a man who slaps a girl.' "

"And he saw that in a comic book?"

"He was a voracious reader of violent comic books."

I glanced at Sylvia but she pretended not to notice. But she knew, like I knew, that the kid in question very well could have seen his pop slap his mom.

The doctor gestured to the children, who were in the various play areas or over in that session of teens with a shrink. He kept his voice low but his words cut like a blade: "Virtually all of these troubled children read comic books."

Virtually every kid in America read comic books. But never mind.

"I wanted you to see firsthand what we were doing here at the Lafargue Clinic," he told Sylvia. "And perhaps interest you in lending a hand here one evening a week."

She'd been hit up for that twice already and we hadn't been here half an hour.

"I'd be interested in talking about that," she said, not quite committing.

"Good," Frederick said, beaming. "And I would be interested in talking to you about assisting me on my column. Could you and Mr. Starr drop by my suite at the Waldorf tomorrow morning?"

"Certainly," she said, then thought to look at me, and I nodded.

Frederick took her hand in his and patted it; nothing

sexual seemed to be in the gesture, but I found it creepy just the same.

He said, "Is eleven satisfactory? Afterward, I could treat you and Mr. Starr to lunch. My patient appointments don't start till one."

We agreed to all that, and were almost out the door when a young Negro kid in t-shirt and ragged jeans, maybe fourteen, came pushing past us. He did not say "Excuse me."

What he did do was get right in Frederick's face and start yelling. Faces all around, kid faces, shrink faces, turned toward the confrontation with alarm.

Sylvia glanced at me, and I glanced back—was this any of our business?

"You told my *mom*!" the kid was saying. "You told my *mom*!"

"Ennis," the doctor said, keeping his cool, "I told your mother nothing. We have what's called a doctor and patient relationship, which is confidential."

"*Confidential*'s a damn *magazine*! You ratted me out, old man! Told her I stole that money she hid!"

"Did she tell you that, Ennis? Because it's not true. I did not betray you."

"I says you did. Now my old man's gonna whup my ass, thanks to you. Well, maybe I'll do somethin' where I gets put away and the old man can't touch me."

Where the knife came from, I couldn't hazard a guess. But first it was like the kid was shaking a fist at the doctor, then there was a *snik* and a long blade was thrust in that Germanic puss, like this patient might give the doc an impromptu nose job.

"Suppose I cuts you? I'm jes' a crazy nigger, right, doc? They puts me in Bellevue and the old man can't *touch* me!"

The kid didn't know I was alive, or anyway he didn't before I latched onto his wrist, from behind, and yanked down his arm and twisted, hard, until the switchblade clattered to the linoleum.

I heard Sylvia gasp as the kid whirled and glared at me with eyes and nostrils flared, but that slowed down his punch, and I doubled him over with a right hand to the gut that kept his punch from even landing.

When he came back upright, faster than I thought he would, he shoved me, pushed past Sylvia, and rushed into the night.

The room was abuzz, but Frederick said nothing. He knelt, picked up the switchblade, which he knew enough about to retract the blade, and dropped it in his lab coat pocket, as if a candy wrapper he'd discard later.

He looked more disappointed than shaken or afraid. "Thank you, Mr. Starr."

"Patient of yours, doc?"

He nodded gravely. "Very troubled boy." He frowned at me. "Would you be surprised to learn he's a comic book reader?"

No, and I wasn't surprised the doc had brought it up, either.

I said, "Where's the phone? I got a cop friend I can call."

"No! No. Let it go."

"Let it *go*? Are you kidding? He'd have cut you if I hadn't taken that blade away from him."

"We can't know that."

I glanced at Sylvia. She looked dazed and said nothing. I wondered if she might not be having second thoughts about helping out here.

"Well," I said, shrugging, "it's your clinic, and your life. See you tomorrow morning, I guess."

He nodded, preoccupied. Dr. Tweed was coming over to consult with his boss when I took Sylvia by the arm and ushered her into the darkness of the alley.

As rats scuttled by us into the garbage, I said, "Yeah. Comic books."

"Huh?"

"All those kids, Syl. Living in poverty and violence and despair, that's where all their problems come from, right? Comic books."

I drove her back to the Village.

Sylvia was set to drop by the Starr Syndicate office to briefly meet with Maggie at ten o'clock before we went over to Dr. Frederick's suite at the Waldorf at eleven. Fifteen minutes early, I came up the rear private elevator, which took me to the gym behind Maggie's office. As I walked across the padded-mat floor, straightening my tie, smoothing my Botany 500 suit coat, I heard a male voice, the door to Maggie's inner chamber ajar.

It took just a moment to recognize Garson Lehman's thin, nasal tones, and since I couldn't imagine I'd be interrupting anything important, I went on in.

Maggie swivelled in her chair, nodded good morning to me, my presence cutting Lehman off in mid-sentence.

"Join us, Jack," she said. Her hair was up, her makeup limited to mostly just bright red lipstick that jarred nicely with her gray suit and white blouse ruffled at the throat. "Mr. Lehman dropped by without an appointment."

That was a dig, but I doubted the Village's Resident Expert on Everything Artistic (and Sexual) would pick up on it. His long dark hair had seen a trim and a comb, his mustache too, and he wore a brown-and-black herringbone sport jacket with a charcoal tie—the look of a man hoping to make a good impression.

Little late for that.

"Good morning, Jack," he said too eagerly. He was sitting in my chair, so I went around him and took the other one.

"Mr. Lehman," Maggie said, "was just wondering if we'd had a chance to consider his offer to write a column for us, on the popular arts?"

"That's right," he said, sitting forward, eyes bright, "something rather more intellectual than you might find in most newspapers these days, but still accessible to the average man. Challenging but with a lot of zip."

If he wrote such a column for anybody, I hoped he'd avoid phrases like "with a lot of zip."

I gave Maggie a look, and she read it properly, and nodded permission.

"I'm afraid we're already picking up a new column," I said. "By a colleague of yours. Dr. Frederick."

Lehman blinked in surprise. "Really? What does he know about the arts?" He must have realized how that sounded, because he immediately covered with, "I mean, he's an authority on comic books and television and other forms of mass entertainment, but in a very narrow way."

Maggie said, "Dr. Frederick isn't covering the popular arts for us."

"In fact," I said, "he's expressly forbidden to discuss his views on comic books, because of our business relationships with several of the publishers he likes to criticize."

Lehman sat back. He had the expression of a student who'd crammed all night but for the wrong subject. "What on earth *would* his column be about, then?"

I said, "We don't discuss the content of columns that are still being developed, Mr. Lehman. I'm sorry."

But Maggie said, "I think Mr. Lehman has a right to have

his question answered, Jack. He did spark the idea for this, after all."

"Yes," he said, distressed, "we *discussed* a column...."

"People throw ideas for columns and comics at us all the time," I said, "like you did at the restaurant the other night. Never amounts to anything."

He frowned. "Well, *this* time it obviously did!"

"Mr. Lehman," Maggie said, "we've asked Dr. Frederick to do a column rather in the style of *Ann Landers* or *Dear Abby*, but with a psychiatric touch. Advice from a genuine authority on human behavior, a recognized expert."

And not a self-styled one like this clown.

Maggie was saying, "Yesterday, Dr. Frederick and I agreed that his emphasis would be on parental problems. Since you helped research *Ravage the Lambs*, you know better than most the extent of his work with troubled children."

Lehman nodded. "Yes. I wrote an article for *Collier's* last year about his efforts at the Lafargue Clinic. Really wonderful what he's doing there." Flushed, he added, "I'm afraid I've embarrassed myself."

"Not at all," Maggie said.

"It's a good subject, frustrated parents and problem children. I believe I could have handled that subject for a column, as well, though I don't have a degree in that field, admittedly."

I didn't figure he had a degree in any field.

He rose. "Forgive me for stopping by unannounced. And do let Dr. Frederick know that if he needs any assistance on the column, I'll be available, as I was on *Ravage the Lambs*."

Maggie and I glanced at each other. We didn't have the heart to tell him.

When he'd gone, I took my proper chair and said, "Maybe we should have thrown him a bone," meaning the ghost job.

Maggie shook her head. "Your Dr. Winters is more qualified. But Lehman dropping in did remind me of something I wanted to show you." From under one of her neat piles she removed a copy of *Collier's* magazine with Danny Kaye on the cover. "Take a look at this."

I did. "By God, that charlatan *did* sell an article to *Collier's*."

"Thumb through. It's a dry run for *Ravage the Lambs*—all about how the Lafargue Clinic deals with children corrupted by comic books."

"That should surprise me?"

"Look at the pictures."

I did. The article about the Harlem clinic was illustrated with full-color staged photos of kids doing terrible things to each other, a boy jabbing a girl's arm with a pen, two other boys tying up a girl to a tree, all the kids probably ten or eleven. But when I said, "full-color," I slightly misstated.

"All these kids are white," I said.

"That's right," Maggie said. "White, well-fed, well-dressed. There's nothing in that article that indicates the clinic is in a basement in Harlem. There's mention of an Episcopal church hosting the facility, but you would never know that the patients were impoverished victims of a notorious ghetto."

I handed the magazine back to her. "So Mr. and Mrs. Caucasian America will assume their innocent boys and girls might be turned evil by comic books, too."

Disgusted, Maggie tossed the magazine to one side—she would have to calm down before it again joined a neat stack. "I don't know whether that misrepresentation is the magazine's doing or Dr. Frederick's. But it smells bad."

"Hey, it stinks. Are we sure we want to get in bed with this guy?"

Maggie arched an eyebrow. "Actually, we'd probably be getting in bed with Dr. Winters, who I'm sure will do most or all of the work."

"Would it be too easy if I said I was fine with getting in bed with Dr. Winters?"

She didn't get the chance to answer that, because Bryce leaned in to say, "Your ten o'clock is here."

Today Sylvia wasn't in one of her sweater-and-slacks combos. She'd be having lunch at the Waldorf, after all, and taking an important business meeting with Dr. Frederick. A rhinestone brooch winked at me, as she traveled the distance from Bryce's door to the desk, her light blue suit sporting a slightly flaring skirt—the effect shapely yet businesslike.

That would please Maggie, whose own gray suit was similar. In fact, Maggie stood and shook hands with Sylvia. I was standing, too. I'm not a complete lummox. But I didn't shake hands with the lovely shrink, just nodded and traded transparently secret smiles with her.

Sylvia's manner had a touch of shy respect in it. "It's a pleasure to finally meet you, Miss Starr."

On the phone yesterday they had a preliminary discussion about her contract, which would be with the Starr Syndicate, though her salary came out of Dr. Frederick's end. But this was their first face-to-face.

"We have every intention," Maggie said, "of making this a successful column, a profitable business enterprise for all concerned. But you *do* know that we have a hidden agenda."

Sylvia nodded. "I've gathered that. And I've been open to

Mr. Starr about my own negative feelings about Dr. Frederick's unscientific approach to his comic-book research."

Maggie reached for a neat pile of folded newspapers, the same pile from which the *Collier's* had been plucked. "I'm sure you're probably aware that my previous profession was in show business."

"Yes, Miss Starr."

I had to grin, but didn't risk a wisecrack. How could Maggie say that with a straight face, in an office with a wall of movie and theatrical posters plastered with her mug and chassis? Or that giant framed Rolf Armstrong pastel of Maggie in feathers and rhinestones, looking down on Sylvia and me, like God with a great figure?

"Well," Maggie said, "these are what we call in the trade the next-morning reviews."

She tossed the papers toward the front of the desk, where we could see the headlines.

Bob Price had made the front page of the *Times*: NO HARM IN HORROR, COMICS SELLER SAYS. The *New York Post* screamed GORE IN GOOD TASTE under the smaller headline SAYS COMIC BOOK KING. And the *Daily News* shouted, AXE MURDER FINE FOR KIDS, CLAIMS COMICS PUBLISHER.

I sighed, looking at the *News* with its juxtaposition of the falling-woman *Suspense Crime Stories* cover with a sweaty-looking, five o'clock-shadowed Price. Worst of all, every story had a paragraph on Bob threatening to murder Dr. Frederick, the "noted anti-comics crusader." At least that hadn't been the lead....

"We're in negotiations with Mr. Price," Maggie said to

Sylvia, "to bring out a comic strip property of his. After this, I don't even know if we can get away with that."

I said, "I'm hoping Frederick's new campaign, against TV violence, will make this yesterday's news."

"Well, right now it's today's news," Maggie said. Then to Sylvia, "Dr. Winters, none of this directly affects you. But I don't want you to go into this under any illusions. I want to be frank with you, but I must have your assurance that what I'm about to share is in strictest confidence."

"Certainly."

"My sub rosa plan is to muzzle Frederick on the subject of comics, by tying him through our syndicate to two of his favorite funny-book whipping boys—Americana Comics and Entertaining Funnies. Once he's signed, I intend to pressure him unmercifully."

"All right," Sylvia said, frowning in confusion, apparently not seeing how she fit into this.

"If the column doesn't do well," Maggie went on, "I will continue its syndication only if Dr. Frederick behaves himself. But he will not know this until after the ink on the contracts has dried. The doctor is a man who may have good intentions, but who is utterly ruthless and unethical in how he pursues them."

"As to comic books, anyway," Sylvia said, "I would have to agree."

"Because of all this, Dr. Winters, I can only guarantee you a one-year contract."

Sylvia's confusion went away and a smile blossomed. Now she got what Maggie was getting at.

"Fine. Understood."

Maggie smiled back at her. "It's nice doing business with an intelligent young woman like yourself."

I said, "I hear men have their uses."

"Yes they do," Maggie said. "For example, you're perfectly suited to escort Dr. Winters over to the Waldorf. You'll be late if you don't leave now."

"Yesterday Harlem," I said to Sylvia, "today the Waldorf. It's a full damn life, don't you think?"

We were in the midst of the mile-long lobby of the palatial hotel—between Forty-ninth and Fiftieth Streets, Park and Lexington Avenues—surrounded by more marble, stone and bronze than in a high-tone cemetery, and more paintings by famous artists than at most museums. The furnishings were 18th Century English and Early American, but the guests were too rich to be impressed. Two thousand such guests were looked after by the same number of hotel staff members.

"You seem to know your way around here," Sylvia said, following me past potted plants and overstuffed chairs.

"Yeah," I said. "Some big-time cartoonists live in the tower suites, which are strictly residential. Hal Rapp lives here, the late Sam Fizer used to."

I decided not to mention that gangster Frank Calabria, who had once been a silent partner of the major's, also had one of those suites, though he didn't live there. His mistress did.

The top eighteen of the hotel's fifty stories were the twin towers, which had their own bank of elevators. We went up to the 35th floor and quickly found 3511, the doctor's suite.

"You know, the Presidential Suite is just down the hall," I said, pointing. "It's where Ike and Mamie stay when they're in town."

She wasn't impressed. "I voted for Stevenson."

"Yeah, me, too."

I pressed the doorbell. It was that kind of hotel, or anyway that kind of suite.

No response.

I tried again, then I knocked good and hard. I did this several times.

Also no response.

I tried the knob. I can't tell you why, other than it was a sort of reflex action after ringing and knocking hadn't got me anywhere. Plus, we were expected.

"It's open," I said.

Sylvia looked at me wide-eyed and I looked at her narrow-eyed.

She said, "Should we go in?"

"The doc may have left it open for us. Maybe he's in session with somebody."

"Dr. Frederick said he didn't take patients till one P.M. And we're right on time." She mulled it briefly. "But…since he's working out of where he lives, maybe he doesn't have a receptionist or secretary. And just leaves it open for patients or expected company. Like us."

"Okay, you sold me." I edged the door open, then looked back at her. "Why don't you stay out here?"

"Why?"

"I don't really know why, but why don't you?"

I had a chill or a premonition or something, and that didn't make me Edgar Cayce: Dr. Werner Frederick had been subject to more death threats lately than Joe DiMaggio. He married Marilyn Monroe, you know.

Moving through the marble-floored entryway, I called out, "Dr. Frederick! It's Jack Starr!"

Nothing, except some echo off marble.

Then I was in the high-ceilinged, long, narrow living room, which echoed other Waldorf residential suites I'd been in—a fireplace at right with facing black leather sofas separated by a glass coffee table; a big picture window on the city at the far end; French doors to a dining room at left (also a door to the kitchen); and beyond the fireplace sitting area, the closed bedroom door. The carpet was fluffy and white, the furnishings modern, everything black and white, solids, no checkered stuff—this leather chair black, that metal lamp black, this leather chair white, that laquer end table black.

Black and white like the doctor's way of thinking. Black and white like the daily comics. The only splashes of color were magazines on the coffee table—one being that *Collier's* I'd just seen at Maggie's. My guess was all these magazines had articles by or about Dr. Frederick.

This was the most sterile, Spartan Waldorf suite I'd ever been in, not even a knickknack or award on the fireplace mantle; but that may have been because the living room had been transformed into essentially his patients' waiting area.

And when I checked the dining room—"Dr. Frederick!"—I found that the area had been converted into an office, complete with a brown leather couch, a desk, swivel chair with tufted leather back and seat, a similar but not swivel visitor's chair, lawyer-style bookcases, everything warmly masculine, reassuring. His desk was as neat as Maggie's—even the stack of vile comic books, for research purposes, made a neat pile.

Okay. So this was where he saw patients.

Because it was handy, I checked the kitchen. Nobody in there, either.

Apparently the doctor had no cook, no secretary, no receptionist. The choice of the Waldorf seemed to have more to do with meeting and attracting upper-class clients than living in comfort. This was, after all, a small tower suite, designed for bachelor living—Frederick was a widower with no children—and he had given up the largest room for his office. His work was his life.

That left only the bedroom, always the most awkward room to enter in a situation like this. I damn near skipped it. I mean, he probably wasn't here, right? Maybe he went downstairs to get his hair cut in the fancy barbershop, or his breakfast in the coffee shop had run late, and like Sylvia said, he just left the door open for us.

Maybe.

The bedroom was Spartan as well. You faced the foot of the double bed upon entering; the bed was modern with a brown spread. Glass doors led onto a balcony—these stood slightly open, and as this was another cool day, it was damn near cold in there. More bland modern furnishing ran to a couple of night stands and a dresser, and another bookcase. Also a smaller work area, a little desk. The only other item of note was Dr. Frederick himself.

He was right in front of me—hanging from a ceiling light fixture by a heavy rope. Eyes rolled back, tongue lolling, dried spittle on his chin, in a lab coat and tie and well-pressed trousers. A chair had been kicked over.

"Oh, *Jack*!"

She was just behind me in the doorway. She had a clawed hand to her mouth, as if about to stifle a scream—and would have been right at home on the cover of *Tales from the Vault*.

So would Dr. Frederick.

I held up a stop palm. "Sylvia, maybe you should wait out in the hall. Whatever you do, don't touch anything."

"We have to get him down!"

She was moving past me and I stopped her, held her by the arm.

"No," I said. "He's dead. No helping him. That makes this a crime scene."

"Well, it's…suicide, isn't it?"

"Yeah, and that's a crime." Which it was, but I doubted Frederick would do any time.

"So what does it mean?" She was doing her best not to come unglued.

"It means the doctor's a piece of evidence now, that shouldn't be tampered with."

"Oh, Jack." She fell into my arms and buried her face in my suit coat. These intelligent women did have a use for a man now and then.

She was shivering, not crying, but upset. I patted her back as my eyes traveled the bedroom. The chair that had been kicked away—either by the doctor to kill himself or a murderer to do it for him—was on the small side. I figured it went with the little writing desk.

She gripped my arm, frightened. "Jack…the *floor*…what *is* that? It can't be *blood*…."

The carpet, more of the white fluffy stuff, was so wet it was squishy, but there was no discoloration.

"Back away, honey," I said. "Just stand in the doorway, if you don't want to wait in the hall."

I knelt. Gingerly I touched two fingers to the dampness and brought them back and sniffed.

"What are you *doing*?"

"Checking to see if it's urine. His bladder might have evacuated when he died."

"...Is it?"

I stood. "No. It's water. And it's cool. Almost cold."

She stepped just inside, tentatively, her intellect taking precedence over her emotions. "Why would the floor be wet?"

I thought I knew. It was crazy, but I thought I might know.

"I need to check something," I told her.

I got a handkerchief out and used it carefully on a rung of the chair.

"You said this was a crime scene! Why are you touching that?"

The chair was upright now.

"Notice anything?" I asked.

"No."

"The doctor is hanging a good three inches above where his feet would have been, standing on that chair."

She came tentatively over, edged beside me, held onto my arm. We have our uses. "Could he have been...on his toes, tying the rope above him, and then stepped off, knocking the chair over as he did?"

"Very damn doubtful."

"Then what *did* happen here...?"

I touched the doctor's hand. "He's cool, but rigor hasn't set in yet. Usually takes three to four hours, unless the conditions are really warm, which speeds it up."

She was hugging her arms to herself. "Or cold and slows it down? It's freezing in here."

"I wouldn't call it freezing. And not cold enough to drastically affect rigor." I added archly, "I mean, we *might* want to check with the *coroner* on this. Still...I wonder..."

"What?"

"There's this old wheeze they use in those 'minute mysteries'—ever read those?"

"Yes, they're sort of puzzles, right?"

"Right. Well, there's one where the hanged man is just dangling in a room with no furniture, and the solution is, he stood on a block of ice. And it melted, and..."

I gestured to Dr. Frederick, who had no opinion.

"Oh, Jack, you can't be *serious*. Why would anyone commit suicide *that* way?"

"They wouldn't. It would be a murder. A particularly sadistic one." I gestured to the corpse, which made a handy visual aid. "You stun or drug your victim, sling him up by that rope so tight around his neck that he can't speak or cry out. Even with his arms free, he can't do anything, the knot's too tight, his every motion hastening his demise. Gradually the ice melts, and your victim is hanged."

"And *that's* why the carpet is wet?"

I pawed the air. "Yeah, but that's just a story. A puzzle. I don't know that it would really work. How does a murderer get a great big block of ice into the Waldorf and up a tower elevator, exactly? Or maybe he comes up the fire escape, carrying the damn thing with tongs. Naw, it's stupid."

"But the carpet *is* wet."

"It is. But maybe..."

"Maybe what?"

"Maybe this *is* a murder, meant to look like a suicide. Maybe Frederick was killed and *then* strung up. The police should be able to tell. Hell, I could probably tell, but I'd have to get cozier with that corpse than would be wise."

"I don't understand."

She was looking at me. She'd been mostly looking at me through this exchange, only occasionally glancing the dead man's way.

"If the doctor was killed," I said, "and the body set down anywhere, even on that bed, while the murderer rigged up the rope and a fake suicide, there will be lividity...a kind of bruising...where the body lay. It's the lowest point where blood collects after the heart stops pumping."

"But where does the ice block fit in?"

"Who says it's an ice block? This is a hotel, isn't it? Ice machines on every floor? A great big heaping pile of ice cubes under the doctor, plus the cool night, might be enough to screw up time of death and the onslaught of rigor. The ice is evidence that melts. I mean, can you prove water soaking a carpet used to be ice?"

"That seems unlikely."

"Doesn't it." I sighed. "Somebody may have gotten very cute killing Dr. Frederick. This killer knew some of the science, but maybe not the lividity part. If the doc's back is bruised, baby, this is a set-up."

Sylvia, quite used to the presence of the dangling doc by now, said, "Couldn't we...check? Carefully?"

"No," I said, and took her by the arm. "I have a couple of phone calls to make."

"The police?"

"Yeah, right after I call Maggie."

I deposited her in the living room on one of the facing couches. She was shivering and I was tempted to light a fire. But I didn't live here, did I? Right now, nobody did.

I used the phone on the desk in Frederick's office, got Bryce as expected, and was put right through to Maggie.

"Frederick's dead," I said without preamble. "Suite was unlocked. We went on in and found him hanging by a rope in his bedroom."

As casual as if I'd just reported picking up theater tickets, she said, "He doesn't seem the suicide type."

"With that ego, he'd have needed two ropes."

"Don't be ungracious, Jack."

"It's almost certainly murder. His feet were three inches higher than the chair. There are some other hinky aspects that I can fill you in on later."

"Do it now."

I did, briefly.

"Dr. Winters is with you?"

"Yeah. She did well."

"I'm not surprised. You know, Jack, you just can't leave this to the police."

"Why can't I?"

"Bob Price is going to be suspect number one, and we're doing business with him—you accompanied him to the Senate hearing. And Dr. Frederick was negotiating with us for a column, in case you bumped your head and got amnesia. None of that's well-known, but it will come out."

"I suppose so."

"Anyway, if Frederick is a murder victim, this stands likely to tarnish the entire comics community. But if you can bring the murderer in, that might cast the Starr Syndicate in a positive light."

"Pretty shaken up by the doc's death, aren't you, Maggie?"

"Like you are. Call Chandler."

She hung up.

So I called Captain Chandler of the Homicide Bureau.

Sitting there in the dead doc's desk chair, I waited for the switchboard at the Tenth Precinct to put me through to the Homicide captain when I noticed the comic book on top of the stack, a *Dick Tracy*. I was thumbing through it idly, waiting for Chandler to come on, when I got to the minute mystery in back.

You know the one.

About a suicide and a block of ice?

CHAPTER SEVEN

Captain Pat Chandler of Homicide had the rugged good looks of a TV cop, which made him all wrong for real life. A broad-shouldered six-feet, Chandler had brownish blond hair and strong features in his narrow face, including piercing sky-blue movie-star eyes and a Kirk Douglas cleft chin.

Hollywood would have done better for him than the rumpled raincoat and formless tan porkpie he sported, which he tossed on the sofa opposite Dr. Winters in Frederick's living room. The pressed blue suit, however, and the striped shades-of-blue tie against his button-down white shirt, looked sharp. Maybe his good-looking better half was doing her housewifely duties, although when a woman looks like a blonde Maureen O'Hara, a guy might be up for ironing his own shirts and getting his own goddamn suits to the cleaners.

I introduced Sylvia to him, and gave him a quick rundown on how we'd come into the unlocked suite and found the hanged man. Very briefly I explained our business here—that Dr. Winters was being interviewed to assist Frederick on a prospective advice column for the Starr Syndicate.

After asking her a few questions, Chandler directed Sylvia to stay put in the living room. Two uniformed men were posted in the hall, but the Homicide captain seemed otherwise alone, no sign of the lab boys yet. We went into the bedroom.

Patiently I watched while he made most of the same deductions I had—the disparity between the chair seat and where the victim's feet reached, for instance. I expected him to haul the doc down, but he was waiting for the forensics team. He noticed the damp floor, knelt to check if it was urine, and so on. He did not make the leap to melted ice, but he did wonder if the room—with those balcony doors open—had been cold enough to screw up determination of time of death.

"Rigor's just starting," he said.

Then he asked me to steady the corpse, which I did, hugging the dead man around the legs and lower torso, so the captain could lift up the white lab coat and untuck the doctor's shirt and check for lividity.

"You can let go," he said.

I did.

"Check this out," he said. He was still holding up the lab coat and the untucked shirt.

The exposed skin was purple, almost black, with lividity.

"Killed and moved," I said.

He nodded. "Probably strangled before he was strung up. If it was *right* before, cause of death gets murky, too. The hanging may have broken his neck. That's supposition, obviously. The coroner will give us a better idea."

"If he was strangled in here," I said, pointing to the writing desk, "maybe seated there, the body could have been moved to the bed while the rope was rigged."

"I'd have to agree. That's consistent with the lividity. What do you make of the damp carpet?"

We'd been getting along just fine, but I had a hunch that was about to change.

"Why don't we go sit down in the doctor's office," I said, putting an amiable hand on his shoulder, "and talk about it."

Chandler glanced around the bedroom, realizing nothing much was to be done until the lab boys and photographers showed. So he followed me through the living room into the dining-room turned psychiatrist's den. Sylvia glanced at us curiously and I raised a hand as if to say, "I've got this."

I took the liberty of sitting behind the doc's desk and Chandler took the visitor's chair. I was tempted to stretch out on the couch, or maybe suggest the captain do that. What I had to tell him was screwy enough for any shrink's office.

I began with the minute mystery notion—he began smirking halfway through—then moved to my own variation, which traded a block of ice for heaping piles of ice-machine cubes.

"Well," he said thoughtfully, his arms folded, an ankle over a knee, "there's no shortage of those in a hotel. You're saying this person knew enough to try to slow down the rigor process and foul up the coroner, and what? Give himself an alibi?"

"Or herself. Certainly muddy the waters."

"But this mastermind didn't know about lividity."

I shrugged. "Lots of people don't. I think our killer is clever, even cute, but…"

His hand was up; if he'd had a whistle in his mouth, he'd have blown it. "*Our* killer?"

I raised both hands in surrender. "Your killer. I'm just the guy who found the body."

"Not the first time. Not even the first time in this hotel."

"Granted, which speaks for my expert status. Mine is an informed opinion, Captain. I think our killer learned about science reading mystery novels and, well, comic books. He or she picked up on slowing down the body's decomposition by cooling it off, but never learned the lividity lesson. But I think there may be even more to it than that."

"Isn't that enough?"

Before he got there, I had opened the *Dick Tracy* comic book to the one-page mystery feature about the man hanged to death in a room without furniture. Though I'd already touched the comic, I'd taken care thereafter not to add any more fingerprints. I used a crystal inkwell to hold the comic book open to the specific page.

"Check this out," I said.

"What?"

"Just do it. Don't touch it, though. Eyeballs only."

He seemed mildly irritated, but got to his feet and leaned over the desk.

"Jesus," he said, his baby-blue eyes tilting up at me. "Where did you find this?"

"Right here on the blotter. On top of this stack." I indicated the pile of horror and crime comics that were apparently evidence the late doctor had collected for his anti-comics crusade. That particular comic was a new kind of evidence now.

"I touched it," I admitted, "before I knew it might have any significance. You have my prints on file to check against any you find. The pulp paper inside won't be helpful, probably, but that slick cover may be."

He sat slowly, almost collapsing into the chair. "What the hell does this mean?"

"It's your case, remember? Your killer."

"Spare me the clowning. You've had time to think about it. And you're part of this nutty comic-book crowd."

"More like comic-strip crowd, but yeah, I think I may have some insights for you. My gut instinct is that somebody staged that suicide with a couple of things in mind. First, if the Homicide Bureau calls it a suicide, no problem. The killer moves on with his or her life."

"But this is a cute, clever killer, you said."

"Yeah. This thing has…levels. The first level is, maybe it gets written off as suicide. Second level is, maybe somebody tried to cool off the body by opening the balcony doors onto an unseasonably cold night, plus piling a ton of ice under the dead man."

"So where does the comic book come in?"

"It's the third level."

"Purpose being…?"

I shrugged. "I figure it for a plant. Somebody official notices this prominently placed funny book on the dead man's desk, and now the Homicide Bureau is taking seriously the possibility that an ice block was used in a very sadistic kill. Suddenly you're looking for a maniac with an ice block, in the Waldorf Hotel! Pretty funny."

"Hilarious."

"But there's another level. A fourth level—if you boys buy the ice block notion, then you start to think the killer is a comic book reader. Maybe one of the kids Frederick worked with. Just last night, I saw a teen hoodlum pull a knife on Frederick at his Harlem clinic."

"Christ, why didn't you mention that?" He was fumbling for his notebook and pencil. "What's the kid's name?"

"Ennis," I said. "That's all I know, but it'll be easy enough to track."

He was writing that down. He flashed me a smile that was almost a sneer. "Of course, suspect number one is going to be your buddy, Bob Price."

"Bob's not my buddy exactly. We were friends as kids. We have mutual business interests as adults. But I do know him well enough to say that I can't see him as a murderer."

"Plus there's some young cartoonist who threatened Dr. Frederick at the hearing…"

"Will Allison," I said. Why hide it? "I can probably get you contact info. Anything to make your job easier, Captain."

He sighed. Tucked the notebook away, and leaned back. Crossed his arms and narrowed his eyes and said, "Okay, I don't mind having you conduct your own parallel investigation, as long as you keep me informed."

"Who said I was going to investigate? But, all right—sure, as long as you do the same."

His grin was almost as rumpled as that raincoat he'd dumped out on the sofa.

A Negro plainclothes dick, Sgt. Jeffords, stuck his head in. "Captain? We informed the chief house detective of the circumstances, as you instructed. And he's here now. Would you like a word with him?"

"Send him in," Chandler said. His eyes found me. "Maybe you better step out, Jack."

"No thanks," I said, leaning back in the swivel chair. "We're keeping each other informed, remember."

He made a face, but nodded.

"Jack Starr!" Bill Griffin said, coming in, grinning. "Don't tell me you found another body? If I were Chandler, I'd check your damn alibi."

He was a skinny five-nine nondescript character in a

nondescript brown suit and hat—the perfect guy for the house dick job at any hotel, but at the Waldorf he was in charge of a small army of ten detectives.

"Treating Jack like a suspect is not a bad idea," Chandler said to Griffin, getting up, shaking the man's hand.

Then the Homicide man sat and so did Griffin, over on the patient's couch. The skinny dick took off his hat and began turning it like a prospector panning for gold. But he already had some gold for us.

"When I heard the suspicious-death victim was Dr. Frederick," Griffin said to Chandler, who'd angled his chair toward the house dick, "I thought I better talk to you."

Chandler's eyebrows went up. "Oh?"

Griffin nodded. His face was so ordinary, you could see him Monday and not identify him in a line-up Tuesday. "I may have a suspect or two for you. If this *is* a homicide."

"It may be a suicide," Chandler said, "but homicide is a strong possibility. Of course, we won't make that determination until the coroner's findings come in. And even *that* isn't for public consumption, okay, Bill?"

"Sure, Pat."

They were on a first-name basis now. Not a surprise—Bill Griffin was an ex-New York cop, as were virtually all the house dicks in town.

"There was a kid last night," he said, wheeling the hat, "a scruffy little nigger kid?"

I said, "I thought you called them Negroes at the Waldorf, Bill."

"Hey, it was a colored kid, black as the ace of spades, rose by any other name. He was millin' around the lobby. Finally, he went to the desk and said he wanted to see 'Doc

Frederick.' The desk clerk said he'd check with the doctor, but really he called me."

I asked, "You were on duty, Bill?"

"Yeah. I work the occasional night. Even big chiefs gotta make like an Indian, y'know, now and then. Anyway, I haul the Negro kid's ass into our office and we frisk him and he has a goddamn *switchblade* on him. These punks! I still got it, if you want it, Captain. The kid was a handful, and kept saying he had to see Frederick, that it was important. Guess what? We showed him to a rear exit and said if we saw him around here again, we'd be turning his black ass in to the cops."

Chandler said, "When was this?"

"I logged it. I can check. I was on till midnight, so it had to be before that."

The timing should have been crucial, but I wasn't sure it was. After all, if the ice trick—whether cubes or block— really had screwed up time of death, the notion of anybody needing, or having, an alibi became problematic to say the least.

Chandler asked, "Did you get the kid's name?"

He nodded. "Ennis Williams."

Chandler glanced at me and I nodded.

"He gave us an address, too," Griffin said. "Harlem someplace. I can get that for you, too."

"Sounds like he was cooperative," I said. "Before, you said he was a handful."

Griffin shifted on the edge of the couch, stopped turning the hat in his hands. "Yeah, funny thing—he was fine with answering questions, but he got worked up when we wouldn't let him see Frederick."

"Did he say why he wanted to see the doctor?"

"That's the funny thing. He said he wanted to apologize! Apologize for what?"

Again Chandler glanced at me. Did we have a murder suspect, or a kid who regretted waving a knife around at the clinic?

"Then there's this other guy," Griffin said, "but it wasn't last night. It was night before last. That was a full-blown incident, lemme tell you."

"So tell me," Chandler said.

"Dr. Frederick called me, or anyway my office. I wasn't on that evening. One of my guys, Ron Matthews? Had to go up there to the doc's suite where this wild man was pounding on the door. My guy Ron says this character was seven sheets to the wind, yelling about 'killing that lousy bastard,' and when Ron tried to walk him away from there, started shoving him. The son of a bitch took a swing at Ron."

"This 'son of a bitch,' " I said. "Did you call the police and have him arrested? That sounds like assault."

"Well," Griffin said, and he gave Chandler an embarrassed grin, "that's the thing. Ron's a big guy himself, and when the guy swung and missed, Ron decked him. So, technically, we hit the guy, and, hell, you both know what kind of red tape we'd get wrapped in if we called that in. So Ron just hauled the bum's drunken ass out and threw him in the alley."

"Who was this guy?" Chandler asked.

Griffin got out a small spiral notebook and thumbed it a page or two. "Name's Pine. Pete Pine."

"Hell you say," I said.

Chandler looked sharply at me. "Know him? Who is he?"

"A cartoonist," I said.

What I didn't mention was that he drew the *Crime Fighter* comic strip spun off from the Levinson Publications comic book of the same name.

A comic strip syndicated by Starr.

Cabs are always lined up outside the Waldorf, and for half a buck the doorman helped us into one. Sylvia was heading back down to the Village. Like the late Dr. Frederick, she had afternoon patients to attend to; unlike him, she'd be keeping those appointments. I made my own appointment with her for supper tonight, and tagged along for eighteen blocks or so, getting out at East 32nd Street, leaving three bucks with the cabbie to cover the whole ride.

Soon I was standing before an unimposing nineteen-story office building that was home to the twelfth-floor offices of Levinson Publications.

The comic book firm's office space was modest, typical glass-and-wood quarters—just a reception area and private sanctums for Levinson himself and his two editors, who were also writer/artists. No bullpen of artists—the rest of the ink slingers, and script scribblers, worked at home.

The receptionist was a busty blonde of maybe thirty-five in a pink sweater and red shift skirt. Pretty if pock-marked, she had the haggard look of the constantly pursued.

Levinson was rarely there, so that pursuit was no doubt the work of those editor/writer/artists—Charles Bardwell and Pete Pine, two skirt-chasing, boozing brawlers, tenement-spawned Dead End Kids not quite grown up, like the Bowery Boys in the movies.

A similar group called "Little Tough Guys" were, not

coincidentally, the sidekicks of Bardwell and Pine's costumed hero, Crime Fighter. Bardwell, a big bossy guy, had his own sidekick in the pint-sized but muscular Pine. The latter's bad behavior was a source of amusement for the former, who egged him on at every opportunity.

The reception area itself was small and drab, with blow-ups of garish color covers of Levinson publications screaming in the otherwise characterless space. These framed oversized covers—*Fighting Crime, Crime Fighter, Crime Can't Win, G-Man Justice*—would have been right at home with the exhibits at yesterday's Senate hearing.

"Is Pete in?" I asked the receptionist, whose name was Ginny. Her makeup was both heavy and haphazard. "Jack Starr to see him."

"I remember you, Mr. Starr," she said, with a faint smile, as if she were recalling the long-ago day when she still could stand men. "Mr. Pine ain't been in today. Or yesterday or the day before, neither."

If you wanted a receptionist who didn't say "ain't" in this town, you hired one with a smaller bosom and stronger defenses.

Pine not being there probably meant he was still on the binge that had included his rampage at the Waldorf, looking to get at Dr. Frederick. That this hot-headed little boozehound drew the comic-strip version of *Crime Fighter* for Starr Syndicate meant he was to some extent my responsibility. I had bailed him out of the drunk tank at the Tombs three times this year, and it was only April, remember.

"Well, is Mr. Levinson in?"

"Mr. Levinson is in Europe. With his wife."

"When will he be back?"

"Not today. June maybe?"

Levinson's absence came as no surprise, either. He was just the bankroller around here, a far-left character branded a Commie by one and all, though his comic-book line had made him a ridiculously successful capitalist. He had done three months for not naming names to HUAC, back in '46, so no wonder he didn't care to be in town for the Senate hearing into the evils of comic book publishing.

Still, Levinson was a nice guy, smart and shrewd, and he even cut his two top men, Bardwell and Pine, in on the profits (*Fighting Crime* alone sold three million copies a month). Consensus in the comics field was that all the publishers should be Commies, if Lev was any example. Not that these drab digs reflected the boss spreading the wealth.

"Mr. *Bardwell*'s in," Ginny said, with eyes deader than Dr. Frederick's.

I hadn't asked if he was. That was because I liked the idea of going into Charley Bardwell's office about as much as this receptionist probably did. But I needed to talk to *somebody* here besides the ill-used Ginny.

So she checked with him by phone and why of course he would be glad to see his pal Jack. Ginny and I traded sighs and long-suffering looks, and I went over and opened the door whose pebbled glass said CHARLES BARDWELL, EDITOR-IN-CHIEF. Who did he think he was, goddamn Perry White?

The office was less than spacious, but it was half-again the size of the reception area, with nice windows onto the city. The plaster walls were pale green with occasional bulletin boards with various paperwork pinned there, printing schedules, cover proofs in black-and-white, full-color printer's proofs; overflow proofs were Scotch-taped to the plaster. File cabinets were stacked with portfolios and loose original art, and stacks of printed comic books were here and there. To that extent it was a typical comic-book editor's office.

The odor that always greeted you upon entering Bardwell's domain, however, was something unique, if peculiarly so, even in this city of smells good, bad, indifferent. This was the middle one. Part of it was cigars. Another part was perspiration. But the secret ingredient, as the ad boys put it, was monkey shit.

I will pause for you to process that information, and assure yourself that you did not stumble upon a bizarre typo.

Against a wall, between wooden filing cabinets, was a steamer-trunk-size cage. Within it were water and food bowls and, on the newspaper lining the bottom of the cage, monkey shit. But no monkey was in the cage, because the creature in question was perched on the shoulder of big, brawny Charley Bardwell, whose back was to me as I came in.

Looking around at me, the monkey was small, scrawny, unhappy, but not making any noise. What variety of monkey this was, I have no idea—organ-grinder type is the best I can do, although it wore no cute little hat nor pants either.

On the wall behind Bardwell's desk was a big color painting by someone other than him (though signed by him) of his character Crime Fighter, a teenager like Batwing's ward Sparrow, who had a pet monkey just like Bardwell's. I had never asked which came first, the comic-book monkey or the shoulder-perched pet. Some questions just can't be answered, like the chicken or the egg, and how the hell did Ed Sullivan ever get a TV show.

As for Bardwell, the big broad-shouldered man—he was

six-four, his build athletic—was seated at his drawing board doing rough pencils for a true-crime cover. He was in a white shirt with rolled-up sleeves, sweat circles, and suspenders.

The monkey showed me its teeth and its wild eyes, but remained relatively silent. Sometimes when you came to visit Bardwell, the monkey was leashed to a leg of the drawing board; if the animal seemed content, everything was fine—but if the animal was nervous, Bardwell was in one of his moods.

Today, the ruddy-cheeked Bardwell appeared in high spirits. He grinned at me over his shoulder, which put his face beside the monkey's (also grinning), and said, "How the hell are you, Jack? Has our strip picked up any new papers?"

"I'm fine," I said. "No new clients but our list is holding strong."

He swiveled toward me, the monkey holding on for dear life, chattering a little (the monkey, not Bardwell). The editor had an oval face with a high forehead and small dark eyes that angled weirdly at the outer corners, giving him a permanent scowl despite frequent toothy smiles. His dark hair was combed carefully to conceal thinning. His nose was a formless lump of clay applied by a careless sculptor.

I sat on the edge of his desk, facing him at the drawing board. I could see past him to his artwork, which was sketchy and fairly terrible. Word was he only did rough layouts and other artists finished the pencils and inks. Like Walt Disney, Bardwell was only good at one thing—his flourish of a signature, which appeared on every cover and the title page of every story he "drew" and "wrote" (a woman supposedly ghosted his scripts).

"I hear you were at that dumb-ass travesty of a hearing yesterday," he said, lighting up a fat cigar with a Zippo. The monkey reacted to the flame about as well as King Kong did to flashbulbs.

"Easy, Buster," he told it.

Buster looked like he (or she) might cry. I thought I might cry myself, thanks to the bouquet of cigar smoke and monkey dung.

"Yeah, I was over at Foley Square," I said, my hat in my hands.

Bardwell wouldn't know about Dr. Frederick's demise yet—way too early for it to have made the radio or TV.

I went on: "They really took poor Bob Price to the woodshed."

"Ha! I'd feel sorry for him if he wasn't such a goddamn thief."

I didn't respond to that. I knew Bardwell considered the Ghoul character who introduced EF's horror stories to be a lift of his own ghostly Mr. Murder character, the narrator in *Fighting Crime*.

"But that Frederick bum," he said, shaking his head, frowning. The monkey also shook its head and frowned. "That quack is a goddamn menace. A rat bastard and a public enemy. Bad enough he doesn't know what the hell he's talking about, he has to make trouble for a bunch of hardworking Joes and Janes! Doesn't he know there's an entire industry out here whose livelihood he's threatening? You should talk to *Pete* on the subject!"

"Yeah? Not a fan of Dr. Frederick?"

"*No!*" He began laughing, loud and hearty, the monkey

looking at him aghast. "Boy, would I like to see Petey get his hands on *that* puffed-up windbag. Little wild man would tear him apart! *That* would be *funny* as hell."

"Pete feels the same way you do about the doc?"

"Oh, God, yes!" He laughed from his gut, rocking his chair; the monkey held on for dear life. "Just the other day? Why, Petey was up here ranting and raving, buckin' for a straitjacket. Saying as how he was gonna toss that clown out a window or tear him limb from limb or some craziness." He shook his head, the permanent scowl fighting his big grin. "You know that cut-up Petey! He's a looney tune, a certified zany."

"I know Pete."

Bardwell gestured with the cigar, the monkey clinging to a suspender. "He says, 'I'll go over to his ritzy office and shove his goddamn couch up his ass!' " This Bardwell found hilarious, and Buster joined in with the laughter.

"When was this, Charley?"

"Yesterday, no, day before yesterday." The big man gestured toward his crude drawing with a thick-fingered, clumsy-looking hand. "It's all a blur, the hours we put in, these crazy deadlines we artists put up with."

As top editor, of course, he set those deadlines.

"So Pine really lost his temper, huh?"

"Oh, God, did he. Standing right there, between where we sit, stomping around like an Indian doing a war dance. But come on, Jack! Don't give me that look. Pete's a proud little guy. He come up from nothing, like me. Really cares about his work. You probably think of him as this roughneck who likes a drink now and then…"

Now and then.

"…but he's an *artist*, man, and all us artists are Bohemians at heart. If you knew him better, Jack, you'd know he's really just a good-hearted lug. Just another sentimental slob like yourself truly."

Bardwell had been penciling a cover on which a wild-eyed maniac was thrusting the face of a screaming woman, her hair already on fire, into the gas burner of a kitchen stove.

"So you didn't take Pete seriously?"

He made a farting sound with his lips; the monkey seemed offended. "Are you kidding? The little squirt was just blowing off steam. Spouting a bunch of b.s."

"Such as?"

"Jack, take it easy. Pete'd had a snootful, *I'd* had a snootful, and we were discussing the man everybody in comics loves to hate." The cigar-in-hand waved at me. "I know, I know, with the comic strip and all, how important Pete Pine is to Starr right now. And if you're worried about him keeping deadline, cause he's off on a bender, well, don't. He has plenty of help on that strip."

I had doubts Pine was drawing *any* of the *Crime Fighter* strip. He was editing three comic books and drawing two more, every month. Though he was a better artist than Bardwell— Faint Praise Department, as *Craze* would say—I suspected he, like his buddy Charley, was mostly just signing the strip.

"Humor me," I said. "What kind of b.s. was Pete spouting?"

Bardwell painted the air with blue cigar smoke. The monkey and I listened.

"Silly, ridiculous horseflop," he said, laughing again, not so loud, but laughing, "about how he was going to go and find that son of a bitch Frederick, and strangle him with his bare hands."

I said nothing.

Bardwell frowned at me. So did the monkey. "What is it, Jack?"

"Somebody killed Werner Frederick."

"Huh?"

"Killed him. Probably last night or early this morning."

He whitened, the cigar dangling from his lips. "Jesus. Hell. First I heard."

The monkey nodded.

"It was murder," I said, "right there in Frederick's suite at the Waldorf. Somebody choked him to death, whether strangled him with 'bare hands' or using a ligature, I don't know. Then whoever it was rigged up a rope and left the old boy hanging. Fake suicide. Took the homicide dick maybe two seconds to see through it."

Bardwell shook his head and Buster mimicked him. "You don't think *Pete*...."

"Pete was at the Waldorf night before last. In a drunken rage, pounding on Frederick's door, yelling out threats."

"Oh Christ...."

"The staff didn't call the cops, just tossed his ass out...but the cops know. The house dick keeps a record of stuff like that."

He made himself smile; it looked sick. "Come on, Jack. You know Pete's all talk."

"No. He isn't. I've exchanged blows with that shrimp myself, trying to help him. While you stood on the sidelines and laughed your butt off, by the way. Where is he, Charley?"

He frowned in thought, then his tiny eyes blazed. "You want to *warn* him? That's *great*, Jack. Should I round up some dough for him? Should we get him out of town? I'll do anything—I love that little guy like a brother."

It occurred to me then that Bardwell always needed a sidekick. Either the monkey on his shoulder or the one he went carousing with.

I climbed off the desk, put on my hat. "I'm helping the cops out on this. Maggie wants me to help clear it up fast as possible, to limit the damage. If I get to Pete first, I can maybe sober him up, and get him to turn himself in."

Bardwell and the monkey thought that over.

I said, "It'll score Pete a few points."

"Well," the cartoonist said softly, "he's probably at his apartment, his studio."

"I'll check there, but I tried his number from the Waldorf. No answer. Where else would he be?"

"…He's been seeing Lyla."

"Lyla Lamont?"

He nodded.

Lyla was a gifted cartoonist, better than Bardwell and Pine put together. But she lived pretty wild herself, down in the Village, and had even lost a syndicated strip over missing deadlines.

That strip had been for Starr, so I knew where to find her.

"Don't call over there and warn him," I said, going out. "I'm going to handle this in the best way possible."

He nodded glumly, but the monkey grinned.

It was pretty funny at that.

CHAPTER EIGHT

A quick cab ride down Lexington brought me to the moderately dingy building where Pete Pine had a second-floor apartment above a drugstore. I pounded on Pine's door but got no response, and—putting my ear close to the paint-peeling wood—could hear nothing beyond.

That didn't mean he wasn't in there—he might be sleeping it off, or ducking loan-shark enforcers or gamblers' goons looking to shake money out of him. I'd seen him wearing their bruises many times before.

So I tried the drugstore downstairs, where the druggist, the soda jerk and the cashier all knew him, though only the cashier (a pretty brunette) seemed to like him at all. He was a regular customer, particularly at lunchtime, often had sandwiches at the counter, but hadn't done so today. Hadn't yesterday or the day before, either.

That cashier was a case in point: women liked the guy. Pete Pine was small but handsome, or anyway handsome enough, with dark curly hair. Whereas his organ-grinder buddy Bardwell had little squinty eyes, Pine had big dark, long-lashed Robert Taylor eyes. When it came to build, he was more Alan Ladd, slight but wiry, and when he wasn't drinking, he seemed shy, quiet, even gentlemanly.

But after a woman became acquainted with Pete Pine, she was as liable to get punched as kissed.

Which was why I disliked the son of a bitch so much. I just don't like men who knock women around. Call me old-fashioned.

Even the cockiest cabbie will admit that the odd-angled streets of Greenwich Village confound him; local residents claim to have no trouble navigating, but the rest of New York remains bewildered.

So my next cab deposited me to fend for myself on Eighth Street, near the Village Barn, a tourist trap, and soon I was walking among coffee shops and bookstores and sidewalk art displays, past females in black tights and bearded males in striped shirts, often paired off, though not necessarily with the opposite sex. We had another overcast, cool day, but everybody wore sunglasses anyway. A lot of dogs got walked down here, so you watched your step, and I was happy to be one of the few sidewalk-trodders not wearing sandals. At least it wasn't monkey shit.

Lyla Lamont lived on one of those cobblestone side streets rife with converted stables and carriage houses. Her building was a three-story brick pile that had been whitewashed, its shutters painted green, ironwork painted black. Similar buildings lined both sides of this narrow street, all overseen by the only gas lamps left in the city.

Lyla was on the second floor. I'd been here a number of times, picking up past-deadline artwork when she was doing her strip *Miss Fortune* for Starr. The strip had been pretty risqué for family newspapers, sort of a female Zorro, and fairly popular, particularly with adolescent girls still working out their sexuality. There were paper dolls, too, with Miss Fortune and other cuties in their lacy underwear, also popular, particularly with adolescent boys still working out theirs.

La Lamont was fairly tall but not willowy, more curvy, an exotic beauty in a Maria Montez kind of way. I would come to the door, she'd be in a black silk dressing robe, smoking a cigarette like Rita Hayworth in *Gilda*, with one pale, perfect leg slipped outside the robe like a dare.

She would hand me the art between big slices of cardboard, say, "Don't scold me," and shut the door. In other words, she would raise my expectations, then immediately lower them. If you said she was a tease, you'd be off by half a compound word.

What a big, plush woman like this was doing with a squirt like Pine, I couldn't imagine. But rumor had it she drank hard and smoked reefer and slept with anybody of either sex who struck her fancy. This might have intrigued me if I hadn't been the guy who had to come around periodically to shake overdue artwork out of her.

The last time I'd opened this green door, up three little steps from the sidewalk, had been two years and a few months ago, right before Maggie fired Miss Fortune's creator for unreliability. I wondered if Lyla had changed much in that time.

I went in and looked up the narrow flight of wooden stairs to the second-floor landing where, *I'll be damned*, there she stood. The first thing I noticed different about her was the lack of a black silk robe.

She was, as the 25-cent paperback writers are wont to say, stark naked.

Stood there pale and white as the flesh of an orchid, her

legs endless, her hips flaring, the waist narrow, breasts high and sweeping outward like a threat paid off by her dark erect nipples, a mane of gypsy curls brushing her shoulders, its raven blackness rivaled only by the startling snarl of ebony below her belly button.

Lack of attire be damned, she seemed poised to come down the steps, apparently in a hurry, her dark eyes so wide they were almost popping, and she was one step down when a second figure flew out on to the landing, a male figure, small, compact, wearing a t-shirt and rolled-up jeans and a face contorted with rage.

Pete Pine.

He shoved her hard from behind, like the guy on the cover of that *Suspense Crime Stories* comic book at the hearing, and she was falling toward me as I hurtled up the stairs. She didn't tumble, she had the presence of mind to grab onto a banister, which didn't stop her fall, her hand sliding down the wooden pole just as she began to do a header, but I was up there in time to catch all that long-legged nakedness in my arms.

For a second, my balance went, and I felt myself tipping backward, and we would have rolled down those narrow stairs in a beautiful demonstration of that classic phrase *ass over teakettle*, but I managed to lean forward and catch myself, hand clutching the banister even as I clutched her.

"Jack," she said, eye to eye with me. She had a throaty alto that went nicely with the rest of the package.

"Lyla," I said.

And I eased her out of my arms and she held onto the banister, and I glared up at the wild-eyed Pine, who was breathing hard, like he'd just lifted a piano. The runt had the fearless look of a madman, but I probably looked much the same—he was like a burning building I was running into, to save a baby, only I didn't want to save this baby. I wanted to throttle it.

I expected him to retreat into Lyla's apartment, but instead the crazy little bastard leapt at me, and then he was on me, smelling like a tavern at closing time, taking me backward, and I went bumping down on my back, keeping my head up so I didn't smack it against the wood, with him riding me, traveling maybe a third of those steps before Lyla put herself in our path, stopping us with her thrust-out bottom as she hung onto that banister with both hands.

Somehow my legs found purchase, a foot on one step, the other foot on another, and shoved up into Pine, with as much force as I could muster, sending him onto his back. I glanced at Lyla and for the first time realized she had blood on her mouth and a bruise blossoming beneath one eye.

He'd been beating her.

A nice little lead-up to shoving her lovely ass down the stairs.

He scrambled off, retreating a step or two, and I got to my feet and reached up and grabbed him by the t-shirt and pulled him forward, then thrust him back, so that his head hit the steps hard. I did that maybe four times, until the wildness went out of his eyes and they started rolling around like marbles.

But even half-unconscious, he managed to kick a powerful little leg out and catch me in the stomach, and I let go of him, reflexively. Again he retreated up the steps. Managing not to puke, I scrambled up after him. As I did, I glanced back down the stairwell at Lyla, maybe halfway to the street now, getting out of our way. Too many fists and feet were flying to suit her, and who could blame her? She just held onto the banister with both hands, her back to the wall, her bare breasts heaving.

In that glance, however, I noticed that she was smiling—blood trickling from the corner of her mouth down her cheek, but smiling as two men fought over her in a stairwell. There was something evil about it. Also, something that propelled me upward where I caught the little prick (that's the missing part of the compound word, by the way) on the landing.

I tackled him and, like a squirming dog, he tried to escape my grasp. A elbow caught me in the side, once, twice, three times, and then he was out of my arms and I was still down there on the wooden platform that was the landing and he was kicking me, in the ribs, in the stomach, not terribly hard because the space was limited and the angle was wrong, but like stings from a persistent insect, the blows took their toll. Finally I caught his foot—he was in tennies—and twisted it and he went down hard on his side.

We got up simultaneously and he began swinging on me, tiny stinging pellets. They were hard little blows, not doing me as much harm as the women he liked to hit, but sharp little smacks, that too, took a toll. He was so close to me that brewery smell engulfed us both. I assumed a traditional fighter's pose, leading with my left, and jabbed him in the chest three times, *bam, bam, bam*. When he paused in his punching, to grab a breath and maybe try for my head, my right fist shot in and turned his face into a smear of red, and he looked like a kid who got into the strawberry jam.

He managed to bring a fist up from his waist and slam me in the temple and, laugh if you want, but I saw stars. Maybe not comic-book stars, but I saw the damn things, and I was woozy on my feet and grabbed onto him in a classic boxer's clinch, to keep my footing.

I don't think I threw him down the stairs. Not exactly. I held him away from me and I shook him and I'm sure, pretty sure, I didn't let go of him intending him to fall. Fairly sure.

But fall he did, windmilling his arms, then doing a somer-sault that looked almost athletic—bouncing off the narrow side walls enough to slow him some—and Lyla made no move to halt his fall or slow it, either. Nor did she scream. Her smile was gone, her expression almost clinical as she watched the little bastard reach bottom, making a sound like a bundle of kindling tossed off a truck. He lay still.

Had I killed him?

Lyla's eyes flashed up to mine.

Have you killed him?

Self-defense. Chandler would back me up, no problem. Then why was I shaking? And if I'd killed him, had I also taken care of the Dr. Frederick problem? Was the doc's death avenged? Not that I cared to avenge that particular death.

Then the little cartoonist got to his feet. He didn't bound up, but he got to them. He stood down there by the wall mailboxes, weaving just a little. Then he seemed to regain himself, and his bloody face sneered up at me and, in a childish display that was damn near amusing, held up his middle finger.

Whether it was for my benefit, or Lyla's, or both of ours, I couldn't tell you.

I thought about yelling down to him that the cops wanted to talk to him. That Frederick was dead, murdered, and he was wanted for questioning.

But why warn the bastard? Even if I'd had the breath left in me to do that....

Then he was gone.

Lyla looked up the stairwell at me. She appeared small, but then she was better than halfway down those stairs. "Are you all right, Jack?"

"Never better," I said, and passed out.

I woke up on a couch in Lyla's living room. She was sitting beside me using a damp, cool washcloth on my face. She'd taken time to wash the blood off her own face, which was understandable. She looked quite lovely. Her eyes had an Oriental cast and her mouth was full and lush and as red as the blood she was cleaning away.

She was also still very naked. Nude.

I once heard a comic in a Village club say that the difference between men and women was that a nurse would bend down to recover a male accident victim's severed arm, while the man with his remaining arm would reach out a hand to fondle the nurse's bottom. Well, "ass" is how that comic, Lenny Bruce, had put it, and his joke came immediately to mind as my eyes fixed themselves upon those thrusting naked breasts, jiggling as her hand worked at soothing my red badges of courage.

"Why don't you put something on," I said, remembering the black silk robe.

"I'm in no rush."

Speaking of rush, all of the blood remaining in me was rushing to one region.

"No, really," I said. "It's distracting. There's things we need to do. And talk about."

"What kind of things?"

"Put something on."

"Party pooper."

She rose. Did I watch her go? The long back tapering to that narrow waist above the dimpled, perfect globes of her bottom. Of course, I didn't.

I sat up.

This was Lyla's living room, and while distinctive and distinctively arty, it was not your typical Bohemian wood-and-block-bookcases, mattress-on-the-floor affair. The furniture was Spanish, stuff dating to the twenties and scuffed up some, but ornate and all to a theme, as opposed to the mix-and-match Early Thriftshop look of most Village pads. The walls were white plaster, though the one opposite where I sat had been painted black, with white, Picasso-ish figures stroked onto it, waving their arms, apparently dancing to some cool cat playing a hot instrument. The fireplace, too, had been painted black. Framed, somewhat expressionistic paintings by Lyla of herself, full figure—she was nude in those, too—rode on the walls. A Hi-Fi squatted in the corner, on the floor. A scattering of LP's ranged from classical to Sinatra.

This nudity bit actually didn't surprise me. She'd always been nude under that silk robe, when I'd previously come calling. And that she posed for herself in a full-length mirror when she was painting or working on her comics was legendary in the business. Half a dozen cartoonists had told of walking into her working space (sometimes at various down-town comic-book publishers' offices) to discover her starkers, looking at herself in the mirror, brush of black ink in hand, her drawing board cranked up to accommodate a standing artist.

Legendary perhaps, but not a legend: Miss Fortune was the spitting image of her creator.

She came back in wearing a red beret.

That's it. A red beret. And a red, devilish smile, and of course yards of ghostly pale flesh. She pulled up a velvet-topped Spanish stool and sat before me with her legs wide, hands on her thighs. Pink peeked out of the thicket at me.

"Better, Jack?"

"Oh yeah. Much."

"I never figured you for a prude."

"Take a closer look. You'll see that was never the case."

"Ah! So I *did* get a rise out of you."

"What the hell's the deal with you and Pete Pine?"

She shrugged, a little chagrined. Utter nudity was no em-barrassment, but admitting to a relationship with Pete Pine was worth being ashamed over.

Couldn't agree more.

"We've been seeing each other," she said, her voice softer, not at all sultry. "Going on two months."

"Has he been living here?"

She shook her head. "I need my privacy."

"Yeah, well, I'm kind of on the modest side myself. What's the attraction?"

"Initially," she said with another shrug, the breasts coming along for the ride, their tips soft now, "it was a work arrange-ment. I ghosted several weeks of that comic strip he's doing for you."

"Is that right?"

The red lips offered up a sly smile. "Didn't you notice the improvement in the art?"

"I don't read that strip. A lot of what we syndicate leaves me cold."

"That sounds vaguely disloyal."

"Reading crap like *Crime Fighter* isn't what I'm paid for."

"What are you paid for?"

"Dealing with trouble that talent gets themselves into. You know, like coming around here and half-getting killed in a stairwell fight, and dealing with a completely crazy broad parading around in her birthday suit. Is the kind of trouble I deal with. Is what they pay me for."

She looked at my lap. "Must be terribly hard work."

Her smile was impish, which didn't play that well. I mean, sirens can't really pull off "imp."

She was saying, "I got a big charge out of ghosting that stupid strip for the very people who so heartlessly killed *Miss Fortune*."

"We didn't kill it. You did. You missed deadlines, and anyway, we'd lost about a third of the papers, as the costumed hero thing passed its peak. Nothing personal."

She crossed her legs. It was almost a relief. "So Jack... what trouble brought you around? I don't work for you anymore, as you've so graciously pointed out."

"I was looking for Pete. Bardwell said he might be here. What the hell was going on? The bastard was beating you. Are you all right?"

I'd been so caught up in the punishment I'd taken, I hadn't thought to ask. I felt about as gentlemanly as Pete Pine.

"I'm kind of used to it," she said, touching the mouse under her eye. She shrugged again. "Pete's a nice guy, when he isn't boozing. And I don't mind it a little rough. I like a man to be a man. But Pete gets mean, when he's got a full tank."

"He's a psychopath."

"Maybe a little." Another bobbling shrug. "I was through with him. That's what the brouhaha was about, us breaking up. He wanted me to do things I wouldn't do."

I tried to conjure what those things might be, but didn't have that good an imagination.

"So, Jack, I'll try again. You weren't just wandering the Village, heard a scuffle, and rode to a damsel's rescue. You were looking for Pete. Why? Why were you looking for Pete?"

"Dr. Werner Frederick."

"What about him?"

"Somebody murdered him."

Her eyes tightened. "I can tell you aren't joking. What does it have to do with me?"

"Nothing. It only has to do with Pete. He was seen at the Waldorf…that's where Frederick had his office…"

"I know it is."

"Pete was seen pounding on Frederick's door and shouting threats the night before last. Drunk as a skunk."

"Dr. Frederick was murdered right there? In his suite?"

"Yes." My brain was finally starting to work again. "Listen, can I use your phone?"

"Sure."

It was in the kitchenette. I got Chandler at the Tenth Precinct almost immediately. I told him I'd had a knock-down drag-out with Pine, but that it had been about me busting up a brawl with his girlfriend, nothing to do with the case, and that I hadn't even got into the Frederick situation with the guy before he split.

"I figure," I said, "he's scurried off to his apartment to patch himself up and maybe sober himself up."

"I'll send a patrol car over to pick him up. You think Pine's a good suspect?"

I touched my temple where he'd belted me. "Oh, yeah. Warn the boys you dispatch that he's a scrapper. If he's not home, check the bars in his neighborhood. Or the bars in the Village—he may not have got any farther than that."

"Thanks, Jack," Chandler said, and hung up.

When I got back into the living room, the beret had disappeared but the black silk gown had come out of hiding. She was sitting on the couch now, a leg crossed, a lovely white limb exposed to remind me what lay beneath the silk.

I sat beside her.

I asked, "Why is it you know that the doc lived at the Waldorf? I don't figure that for common knowledge."

"I was a patient of his."

"*What?*"

She was as matter-of-fact about this information as she'd been lolling around in the altogether.

"I was a patient of his," she said, "for just a short while. He had no idea that I worked in the comic book field. I went to him out of a kind of…perverse curiosity. I told him I was an artist, that I often dealt with images of violence and sexuality, and I wanted to know if something was wrong with me."

"If you don't mind my asking, what was his diagnosis?"

"That was why I stopped going to him. I felt he was…not so much a hypocrite as a shallow thinker. Because I presented myself as a fine artist, whose work appeared in galleries, he saw nothing wrong with my subject matter. I once asked him casually about comic books, and he obviously had a fixation on them, on *all* of the popular arts. He was that typical pompous upper-class intellectual who wasn't worried about what he and other refined types read or saw, but only what the lesser folk read or saw."

I frowned at her. "You knowing Frederick, that may come back to haunt you."

"Why is that, Jack?"

"You're a comic book artist. You went to see him under false pretenses. You knew where he lived, were someone he would likely open the door for. Sweetie, you're a suspect."

She shook her head, all those black curls shimmering. "I didn't do it."

"Didn't say you did. Don't think you did. But the cops will want to talk to you."

"Well…they would have anyway."

"Why's that?"

She smirked humorlessly. "That was why Pete and I were fighting. He wanted me to say I'd been with him, holed up here, for the last two days. Working, drinking, whatever, but *here*, with *him*."

"He wanted you to provide him an alibi."

The Oriental eyes flared wide. "*Now* I realize that. He didn't say why he wanted me to lie for him. My wanting to know why just made him madder. Like you said, Jack, he's a psychopath."

I put a hand on her silk-clad shoulder. "I'll put in a good word for you with Captain Chandler. He's the Homicide dick in charge. Friend of mine."

"That's sweet of you, Jack." She played with my hair. "What's wrong with me, anyway? Why don't I go after nice guys like you?"

"Oh, I used to be a drunk myself. Probably damn near as ugly a one as Pete. But I never hit a woman in my life."

She slipped her arm around me and her face came toward mine and, bruised or not, hers was as lovely a face as I ever saw. Her lips found mine and lingered, hot, moist, sticky with lipstick, her tongue darting, and she whispered, "I like you, anyway."

This time her nakedness was my fault, because I slipped the robe off her shoulders, and filled my hands with those breasts and then reached down to cup one luscious cheek of her bottom. No, her ass. We necked and grabbed each other in various interesting places for a while and it was getting hot and heavy when I stupidly asked, "What did you see in that shrimp anyway?"

"Oh, that's easy."

"Yeah?"

"He's hung like a horse."

Well, that broke the mood. Don't think it was my lack of confidence in being able to compete, but I just suddenly felt I had to get the hell out of that pad with its black wall and Spanish furniture and naked hostess.

I did give her another kiss before leaving, saying, "Maybe another time."

She was still on the couch, nude and confused when I went. I wasn't in the mood to play. She would just have to find some other innocent jerk to seduce.

CHAPTER NINE

Around three-thirty that afternoon, a cab dropped me at the Starr Building. From the street I went into the postage-stamp entry area adjacent to the Strip Joint. We were still using an elevator man, for security if nothing else, and he took me up to the third floor. The small pale-walled, brown-carpeted landing offered two doors, one to a fire exit, the other my apartment.

The apartment, by the way, was a box-car affair with a windowless living room outfitted with Bauhaus-type modern furniture. The off-white walls were arrayed with framed original comic-strip art, black-and-white Sunday pages— Gould's *Dick Tracy*, Herriman's *Krazy Kat*, Sterrett's *Polly and Her Pals*, with a sprinkling of Starr Syndicate stuff, including *Wonder Guy* and *Batwing*. Maybe I should have asked Lyla for a *Miss Fortune*, but the timing hadn't been right.

Now and then visitors to my bachelor pad found my pre-ferred artwork odd, although everyone was impressed by the size of things, which were drawn twice-up before repro-duction. The major used to say that the best comic-strip art was at least as good as anything the modern-art crowd ever whipped up, and even if he was wrong, I couldn't exactly afford a Chagall or Picasso. Getting a great comic-art piece was a snap—all I had to do was ask the artist for one. I was in the business, after all, so complying was a courtesy. And the artists always felt complimented.

The bedroom beyond did have a couple of non-comics, ersatz modern masterpieces I'd picked up in the Village. Another windowless room, this was home to yellow walls, Heywood-Wakefield furnishings, a small desk with a phone, and the bed, a double (ever the optimist).

Next in the chain was the kitchen, modern and white and too big for a bachelor, though it served as decent space for the weekly poker games I threw for newspaper and show biz buddies. This was where I headed, as I hadn't managed to eat anything yet today, and made good on half a pastrami and Swiss cheese sandwich with half-eaten dill that I'd brought home the other day from Lindy's. I had a third of a bag of potato chips handy, so I grabbed a Coke and sat at my Formica-topped table, quietly enjoying the food, my aches and pains taking a back seat.

Still, I was hurting. The scrap with Pete Pine up and down those stairs had resulted in no broken bones, but I had bumps and bruises to spare—even a naked nurse like Lyla Lamont offering a soothing damp cloth, among other soothing damp things, couldn't make those disappear.

I had a date with Sylvia tonight, for supper, and I decided that I'd done enough work for one day. Dr. Frederick would likely still be dead tomorrow. I could pick up then.

My intention had been to clean up a little and go upstairs and report in to Maggie, but as I sat there chowing down, I noticed that my suit coat sleeve was torn (*goddamnit*) and the breast pocket had some stains that might have been ketchup but weren't. I would need to change.

This led to a shower, which turned into something long and luxurious, the hot needles feeling so very good on the sore spots. I leaned both hands against the shower stall wall with my back to the spray and just let the heat have at me.

The bathroom was just off the bedroom, so when I was toweled off, the first thing I saw was the bed, and I forgot about checking in with Maggie and just flopped there, nude as a grape. Nuder. Nude as Lyla Lamont.

Took quite a while to fall asleep, maybe fifteen seconds, and the last thing I remember thinking was how I really ought to set the alarm, to keep from being late for my date with Sylvia.

When the phone rang, I sat up like a cannon had gone off, figuring that it was Sylvia calling, and that I'd slept through supper. I scrambled over to the phone at my desk and plopped down there, working up an excuse and an apology (which would not include anything about jaybird Lyla trying to seduce me). Without windows in the place, I had no context other than the nightstand clock...

...which said four.

This I assumed to be four in the morning. So it wouldn't be Sylvia, not at that hour. Maggie maybe, with some other crazy development in the case?

It was Captain Chandler.

I asked, "What the hell are you doing on the job at four A.M.?"

"Are you kidding? It's four in the afternoon. You finally fall off the wagon?"

I had slept maybe fifteen minutes.

"We picked up that Pine character," he said without waiting for a response.

Fifteen minutes or not, my mind and mouth were sleep-fuzzy. But I managed to say, "Good. What's he got to say for himself?"

"Not much. He was drunk and abusive. He took swings at the uniformed men who picked him up, and he may do some time for it. We frown on people throwing punches at police."

"You've always been a stickler. You got him downstairs in the drunk tank?"

"No. This boy's a champion nutcase. I had him shipped to Bellevue for observation, not to mention drying out."

"So you won't be questioning him till tomorrow?"

"Right."

"Well, he's not going to have an alibi," I said, "unless he finds one in the nuthouse." And I filled him in on Pine's reported attempt to threaten Lyla Lamont into covering for him.

"Maybe he's our man," Chandler said.

"I would love that, I really would. He's a nasty piece of business, and someday he may really kill somebody."

"What do you mean…'really' kill somebody?"

I sighed. "I just don't think he's smart enough to try all that cute stuff at the doc's suite, the ice, the fake suicide, the funny book with the ice-block minute mystery."

"He's a writer, isn't he?"

"Artist. A mediocre one, but professional enough. But let's assume Pine *is* smart enough to pull that muddy-the-water crapola at the crime scene. Smart enough to do that *drunk on his ass*? He's been on a bender for days."

A long pause preceded Chandler saying, "I hate it when you're right. But he's still a suspect. We know he threatened the life of the victim several times, he has no alibi, and he's violent."

I touched my chest where Pine had pummeled me with

his hard little fists. "He is at that. What about that Negro kid—Ennis Williams?"

"I already shook him loose." Weariness fought frustration for control of Chandler's voice. "The kid's mother said she sent him to the Waldorf to apologize to the doc, like her son says. She says Ennis came home right after."

"Of course, she's his *mother*...."

"A neighbor saw him leave, and get back. There remains the possibility that he sneaked out in the night and returned to the Waldorf, but that's pretty thin."

"What does the coroner say about time of death?"

"Nothing final, but indications are the killer did manage to screw that up to where we have an awfully big window for the murder. That ice, depending on the size of the block or the amount of ice cubes, could take anywhere from four to six hours to melt, the coroner says. Jack, we're not much farther along this afternoon than we were this morning."

"What's next?"

"I'm heading over to Entertaining Funnies. I called ahead and warned them to stay put—I mean, it's Friday, they might knock off early for home otherwise."

"They're still there?"

"Still there. I'm planning to leave for there as soon as I hang up."

I thought about that. "Listen, why don't you find something else to do for half an hour or maybe forty minutes?"

"Why?"

"I'd like to head over myself and talk to Bob Price before you do."

"Oh, you would?"

"Remember how we're working together? On separate

investigatory tracks, because I'm part of this funny-book world, which gives me access and insights you do not possess?"

"Yeah," he grumbled, "I remember something like that."

"Let me talk to Bob and his pal Feldman—Feldman's still there?"

"I didn't ask," Chandler admitted. "It's Price who's the suspect, but I did say nobody was to leave."

"Well, Price and Feldman are tied at the hip. Feldman will likely be on deck. Let me talk to them both. I may get things out of them you can't. Then you show up, maybe haul them in for a less friendly questioning, and working both ends we might just get somewhere."

"But you'd like to *clear* Price, wouldn't you?"

"Not if he's guilty. What I *want* to 'clear,' Captain? Is I want to clear this up. Fast. It's bad for the comics business overall, and it stinks for the Starr Syndicate."

"And here I thought you were just being a good citizen," Chandler said.

"Well?"

"If I let you do this, you can't let Price or anybody know any details about the crime scene. We've kept a lid on that—it's a 'suspicious death.' "

"Understood."

"Nothing about faked suicide or blocks of ice or *anything*. Got it?"

"Got it."

Another very long sigh. "I have paperwork that could stand doing. I'll leave here in forty-five minutes. With travel, you should have a good half hour with Price, and Feldman, if he's there."

"I appreciate this," I said.

"Did I mention it was Friday? And that I get off at six? And that you're adding forty-five minutes to my day?"

"Your good-looking wife will understand."

"I hope so."

"She will," I assured him.

No sarcasm, no wisecracks. Chandler was doing me a favor. And probably himself, but he couldn't be sure.

I put a blue blazer on over a light blue Banlon shirt and gray slacks, anticipating my night in the Village with Sylvia, grabbed my hat, and headed back down to the street.

No cab this time. I got the convertible out of the parking garage on 44th and headed over to 225 Lafayette Street and the offices of Entertaining Funnies. The outside of the building, a Greek Revival number, was impressive enough, and the gilded, high-ceilinged lobby, too. But the ten floors above were strictly wood-and-glass office space.

I took the elevator to the seventh floor and moved quickly down the long hall to the far-end suite where a pebbled glass door bore the familiar circle logo with EF within, under which were the words ROBERT PRICE, PUBLISHER.

The receptionist, Betty, a pretty brunette who was engaged to Bob—a rather more aboveboard arrangement than Ginny's with her boss Bardwell back at Levinson Publications—sat at a desk in a small undecorated reception area.

She smiled upon seeing me, blurting, "Jack!"

But that smile disappeared and her expression turned glum as I approached her desk. She stood and came around to offer me her hand, which I took. She wore a pale yellow short-sleeve sweater and a dark green skirt.

She said, "We're all just sick around here about the news."

"The news?"

"Yes. About Dr. Frederick's passing."

She seemed genuinely saddened. You would have thought Frederick was the family doctor or maybe her uncle, not an egotistical bluenose who had made miserable the lives of everyone at Entertaining Funnies. Including and especially her fiancé.

"That's why I'm here." I said. "I want to talk to Bob about it. I know this is late on a Friday, and Hal may be gone, but—"

"No, Mr. Feldman is still here. He and Bob are in the lounge. They're waiting…" She lowered her voice, keeping things confidential though no one else was in the small reception area. "…waiting for the police to come. We had a call. A Captain Chandler is on his way, I guess to question them. It's so terrible, so disturbing."

She looked on the verge of tears, but apparently was too professional to succumb.

I gave her a small, encouraging smile. "Chandler's a good man. Friend of mine. Nothing to worry about. Lounge is through here, right?"

She bit her lower lip and nodded. "Right."

Cute kid. Busty blonde Ginny had her points, and so did Lyla Lamont for that matter; but give me a smart cookie like Betty any day.

Bob Price and Hal Feldman were sitting on a secondhand couch in the small lounge. Both were smoking. Paper cups of coffee shared space with overflowing ashtrays on the scarred-up coffee table before them. The room was a warm, friendly, funky space, with racy, unprintable in-house cartoons plastered to the wall, all caricaturing Price, Feldman and their regular artists. On the wall behind the couch was a big blow-up of a *Craze* cover. A life-size poster of Marilyn Monroe spilling from a bikini was nailed up with a caricature of artist Craig Johnson peeking over her shoulder lasciviously. Several wire racks of the latest EF Comics were here and there, as was lots of secondhand furniture. What came to mind immediately was a faculty lounge at a small-town junior college.

And once-and-maybe-future science teacher Bob Price, in a white short-sleeve shirt with bow tie and baggy brown trousers, looked like the students had been giving him a particularly bad day.

"Jack," Feldman said, smiling, putting out his cigarette in an ashtray despite its overflow. "Nice to see you. Come in. Sit down!"

Price's second-in-command was snappily dressed as usual, gray suit with flecks of black, black-and-white-and-gray patterned tie. He was the kind of guy who'd be jaunty on the deck of a sinking ship, helping the women and children into the lifeboats.

I sank into a comfy if threadbare armchair facing them. "Betty says you fellas know about Dr. Frederick."

Feldman said, "Just that he's dead. That he died under suspicious circumstances."

"Newscaster said," Price put in, "it might be suicide. God, I don't even know what to think."

"You don't?"

He gestured with open hands. "Is this a good thing for us? Or a bad thing?"

"Well, it's a bad thing for Frederick."

"It's not good for anybody," Feldman said gravely.

"Frederick's already done his damage. That *Ravage the Lambs* is a nasty genie that won't go back in the bottle. And hell, maybe he'll be a martyr now."

"I don't mean to callous," Price said, "but he was an awful man. A real enemy to everybody here at EF. When somebody tries to put you out of business, you don't have much sympathy for his problems."

"He doesn't have any more problems, Bob."

He swallowed thickly. He looked pale except for his five o'clock shadow. He looked lousy actually, like he hadn't been sleeping. Had he been up doing a project last night? Working on a story with Feldman, or maybe a solo effort, a typical *Suspense Crime Stories* yarn with a snap ending, maybe? Like the one about the shrink who said everybody was sick sick sick, then hanged himself?

"Maggie's having me look into this," I said.

Feldman was smiling, he almost always was, but his eyes weren't. "Isn't that the police's job, Jack?"

"They're on their way here now!" Price blurted. He seemed damn near as nervous as he had testifying.

"Betty told me," I said with a nod. "The captain of Homicide is a decent guy. His name's Chandler."

"Like Raymond," Feldman said.

"Like Raymond, only not like the corrupt cops in those private eye novels of his. *This* Chandler's a good man, fair as they come—you're gonna want to be straight with him."

Feldman asked, "Does he know *you're* looking into this?"

I thought about dodging that, but said, "Yes. He knows I'm in the business and that I know the players. He thinks I may be able to help. Hope I can."

Price asked, "Are there any suspects?"

I just looked at him.

Feldman did the same.

"Well," I said, "they picked up Pete Pine today. He's been going around town bragging about how he was going to strangle Frederick. But they haven't interrogated him, because they dumped his ass in Bellevue, to dry him out. He's been on a two- or three-day binge."

"Imagine that," Feldman said with a smirk.

"Who else do they suspect?" Price asked.

I laughed, shook my head. "You do remember, don't you, Bob, threatening to kill Frederick in front of a bunch of reporters?"

His smile was sickly, his eyes glazed behind the black-rimmed glasses. "Nobody took that seriously! That's just an expression. A figure of speech."

"Not when the guy you said it about is murdered the next day, it isn't."

Price and Feldman exchanged worried expressions. Had they discussed the probability of Price being targeted by the cops for this? Had Price been disingenuous when he asked about who the suspects might be?

Feldman asked, quietly, "Is it murder, Jack?"

I leaned back in the comfy chair. "I'm not in a position to go into detail. I've been asked by Captain Chandler to keep what I know to myself, for now. But I was at the scene."

Price's black eyebrows were standing damn near straight up, like India-ink exclamation points. "This Captain Chandler, he called you to the scene?"

"No. I found the body."

They didn't know what to say. Price stubbed out a cigarette and got a new one going. Feldman just leaned back, folded his arms, and watched me like I was a news commentator on TV with an important breaking story.

"I can tell you it was murder," I said. "Of that I have no doubt. And I can tell you he was likely killed sometime between midnight last night and seven this morning."

"We were together last night," Feldman said quickly.

Price had no expression at all, though his mouth hung open a little, making him look vaguely idiotic, like the caricatures of him that appeared in *Craze* and in the in-house ones taped to the walls.

"Be more specific," I said.

Feldman continued to take the lead. "We were working on springboards till the wee hours, part of it in Bob's office, part right here in the lounge. Take a look at the ashtray, if you want evidence."

I didn't comment on the quality of that evidence. I asked, "What's a springboard?"

"Oh. It's basically an idea for a story."

"A plot?"

"Not that detailed. We just come up with a premise and a surprise ending. Some ironic way for the villain to get his."

Like the one about the shrink who said everybody was sick sick sick, then hanged himself....

"You didn't work on 'springboards' all night, did you? You surely went home at some point."

Feldman said, "My apartment's only a few blocks from here. When we work late, we go over there and sort of collapse. I've got a couch that Bob's spent more time on than I have."

"You're not married, are you, Hal?"

"No. Why?"

"So there's no little woman to confirm this. Did anybody see you? Getting home at, what time?"

"Probably three A.M. I guess not."

"Anyone else working here at the office last night? Any artist or writer?"

Feldman shook his head.

"Did you take a coffee break and maybe hit the all-night deli down the block? Or have anything delivered?"

"No," Feldman said. He pointed to an old refrigerator, chugging in the corner. "We ate here."

Price finally said something: "Are we in trouble, Jack?"

Are we *in trouble…not, Am* I *in trouble…*

"It would be nice if you had any kind of witness," I said, "to this after-hours story session. Or to getting home afterward. You guys are not just partners, but close friends. Somebody's gonna say one of you is covering for the other."

Softly Price said, "You think Hal's covering for me?"

"No."

Feldman asked, "Or vice versa?"

"No."

Neither guy had the makings of a murderer, not in my book. My only hesitation was the cute, clever nature of the killing—either one or both were the only suspects so far who seemed capable of coming up with such a wacky murder scheme.

"There's a better suspect than Bob," Feldman offered.

I was thinking, *You mean, you?*

But I said, "Love to hear it."

"Vince Sarola."

Sarola was the owner of Independent Newsstand Services,

one of the two major comic-book distributors. He had mob ties, although not to Frank Calabria, who was connected to the rival Newsstand Distribution, Inc. Americana Comics was aligned with the latter, while Entertaining Funnies and Levinson Publications had distribution through the former.

"I don't think so," I said.

Feldman's grin was sly. "You don't think Sarola has a motive? Our sales are down, thanks to Dr. Frederick. And I hear Lev's titles really took a tumble. Down from three million copies for their top titles to under two."

"No," I said. "This wasn't a mob hit."

Price asked, "What makes you say that?"

"None of the earmarks."

Feldman frowned. "How so?"

Well, of course, I couldn't answer him without getting into the killing itself, and I was trying to find a way around that when Betty stuck her head in.

The pretty brunette looked frazzled. "Bob…Hal. Excuse me. But I have Will Allison out here. He's very upset. Wants to see you."

Bob seemed about to grant permission when Allison came pushing by Betty, saying he was sorry but almost knocking her over. She rolled her eyes and shut the door behind her.

The kid was in his *Wild One* get-up, black leather jacket, t-shirt, jeans. His narrow handsome face was overwhelmed by that massive, greasy duck's-ass haircut.

The tall skinny trembling figure, on the brink of tears, stood in front of the seated Price and Feldman like a lowly, loyal subject before his rulers.

"Can you guys front me some dough?" he asked.

Again, Feldman took the lead. "Why, Will? Sit down, sit down, tell us about it."

He swallowed and sat in another secondhand comfy chair across the coffee table from them. He wasn't exactly sitting next to me, because the chairs were spaced apart and angled in. We had met briefly but he didn't acknowledge me or even look my way.

"I gotta get out of town," he said. "Man, I gotta split *right now.*"

Price asked, "Is it this Frederick thing?"

He nodded, the pompadour bouncing. "I threatened the guy, right there in court!"

Hadn't been court exactly, but he did threaten the doc, all right, in a very public place.

"I got no alibi," he said. "Not a damn thing!"

I said, "How do you know that?"

His face swung toward me and he blinked, as if noticing my presence for the first time. Maybe that was the case.

"I'm Jack Starr," I said. "We met the other night."

"Uh...I remember." He looked at Feldman. "Can I talk in front of this guy?"

Feldman nodded.

"Will," I said, "I'm friends with your shrink, Dr. Winters."

"My shrink, too," Price noted quietly.

"So you know my shrink?" the kid sneered, but it was all show. "So what?"

Feldman asked, "What good will money do you?"

The kid jerked a thumb over his shoulder. "I got my motorcycle out front, and I'm gonna hit the road till this blows over. I didn't *do* this thing! I'm innocent!"

"How do you know," I repeated, "that you don't have an alibi?"

He frowned at me, confused, veins standing out on his forehead. "Huh?"

"Time of death hasn't been established, much less announced. How do you know when the doctor was killed? For that matter, how do you know he *was* killed? He might have committed suicide."

Allison stared at me agape.

"Take your time, son," I said.

He swallowed. "Well, the radio said, 'suspicious death.' I figure that's murder. I mean, is it any surprise somebody in our business would kill that guy? I don't mean he deserved it, nobody deserves to get killed, but…he was killing our *business*."

"I wouldn't share that thought with the police," I said.

He sprang to his feet. "That's why I need some *dough*! I need to split! They'll toss me in the can. They'll fit me up for this! If I'm gone, they'll look somewhere else. And then I can come back."

Feldman was shaking his head. "We don't have any cash in the office. I couldn't give you any if I wanted to."

"Okay, okay. How about this. I'll work for you by mail. I'll move around, one post office box here, another there, I got wheels, I can do this."

I said, "Tell me about your lack of alibi, Will."

Exasperated, he turned toward me again. "I live with my mom. In Manhattan. My dad's dead. We got an apartment, and…"

He was floundering.

"Is your *mom* your alibi?" I said. Maybe he'd figured out that a boy's mother is not the best witness.

"That's just it," he said. "She's out of town. Visiting my aunt. I was home alone, working on pages for these guys…" He jerked a thumb toward the couch where Price and Feldman sat. "…and I haven't stuck my head out of there since that courthouse deal."

"No contact with neighbors during that time?"

"No!" He returned his gaze to the publisher and editor. "Fellas, you *know* I'm good for it. Have you got *any* cash on you? Just for gas and food. I know I'm not always reliable on deadlines, but picture this—I'll be on the move, hiding out, keeping my head down. Nothing to do but pencil and ink pages. What do you say?"

I said, "Will, you need to go to the police of your own volition. Flight is an admission of guilt."

"But I'm not *guilty!*"

"Then," Captain Pat Chandler said from the doorway, two uniformed men behind him, "I wouldn't flee."

CHAPTER TEN

The Kaiser-Darrin was parked on Lafayette. I'd left it with the top up because leaving a convertible top down on any Manhattan street was a gamble. I had the driver's side door unlocked when a big beefy hand slid to open it for me.

"Allow me," the low rumble of a voice intoned, or something to that effect. He had the diction of Demosthenes before he spit the pebbles out.

Like his hand, my new friend was big and beefy, a hooded-eyed ex-pug with the standard-issue misshapen nose, puffy scarred-up lips and cauliflower ears. His suit fit him well enough, either tailored or from a big-and-tall shop, but the bulge of a hip holster hadn't been accounted for. His hat was on the snazzy side, a light green porkpie with a darker green-and-red feather. Perfect for the hood about town.

"Have we met?"

"No. I work for Mr. Sarola. He asks in a nice way that you drop by. You drive. I'll ride."

I just looked at him. This was a city street and if I were to shut this thing down, now would be the time and place.

"This is a friendly invitation," the guy said.

"Well, if it's friendly, how about you give me the address and I drive myself over?"

He shook his head, just slightly, but enough to make his point. "It ain't *that* friendly."

Like a hitchhiker you would not in a million years pick up,

he jerked a thumb over his shoulder. Parked behind me was a big green Nash from the late '40s with another big, beefy guy at the wheel, another probable ex-pug, with features so flattened somebody might have hit him in the puss with a garbage can lid. Repeatedly.

"You got an escort," he explained.

Two escorts, actually. The thug (and that's what he was) who would ride with me, and the other thug who would follow along.

Down just two cars behind the Nash—these gangsters seemed to like the '40s models better than the less-sinister '50s ones—a police car was parked, and behind that Captain Chandler's unmarked vehicle, a blue Ford I knew well. If I stalled long enough, maybe Chandler would be down with Will Allison and possibly Price and Feldman, on the way to the Tenth Precinct, and I could attract his attention and find a way to decline this "friendly" invitation.

"You get in," the beefy guy said. "Unlock the door on my side. No funny business. Even Uncle Miltie don't make me laugh."

"Even in a dress?"

No reaction.

Okay, so no funny business. I slid in behind the wheel and unlocked the door on his side. I was not wearing a gun—I rarely did—and no other weapon was hidden away in the glove compartment, either. The only thing I had in common with those well-armed private eyes on TV was the license in my billfold.

The guy was almost too big for the convertible, and he had to take off the feathered hat to keep from smashing it, which actually was fairly comical, despite his ban on funny business. I might have smiled if I wasn't getting taken for some kind of ride, probably not the permanent variety, but a ride nonetheless. And suffering the indignity of providing my own car and driving my own damn self, at that.

The address was in the Printing District, which was centered around Hudson and Varick Street, near the Holland Tunnel. Not much of a ride really, but an agonizingly slow one at rush hour. I made several unsuccessful attempts at conversation ("Any idea what Mr. Sarola wants to see me about?" "What name did you box under?") that got nowhere. When we finally arrived, the massive brick warehouse took up half a block, with enough wear, soot and fade to date back to the turn of the century. An automatic door went up, big enough for several good-size trucks to enter side-by-side, and both my little convertible and the big ugly Nash rolled in. The door closed behind us.

The warehouse was not bustling. This was after five o'clock, and the place was just a big, high-ceilinged box, its darkness interrupted by conical lights hanging high up, with boxes and bundles of comic books and other periodicals stacked everywhere. Walls of the boxes were at the right and left of where we'd parked, and up ahead was another wall of boxes in front of which sat a massive ancient desk with a banker's green-shaded lamp on it and a man seated behind it.

The man was Vince Sarola.

Sarola was a big guy, not as big as his goons but big enough—let's just say he never had a need for shoulder pads in his custom suits. He was natty, as so many top gangsters are, this afternoon wearing a light green tropical suit with a pale yellow shirt and green-and-yellow tie; even his dark complexion had a greenish tinge, or maybe that was the lamp.

He bore a massive head with naturally dark, wavy hair that he kept glisteningly immaculate. His eyebrows were heavy slashes from a charcoal pencil riding a slightly protruding forehead, his eyes dark and large, his nose well-formed but big, his lips thick, grooves of past dissatisfactions making vertical lines in his cheeks. He had a prominent facial mole low on one cheek, and yet he had a brutally handsome look. That had helped a parade of chippie mistresses, over the years, put up with him, that and his dough.

Nobody held onto me as I walked over to Sarola, who smiled at me like I was an old friend who'd dropped by, and rose to extend a hand across the desk, which was cluttered with various bills of lading and other paperwork. But I could hear the hollow echo of footsteps on cement of the big men following me.

I shook with Sarola, who had a skillet of a hand; he sat, and so did I, in a hard wooden chair that had been waiting. It was cold in the warehouse, but not freezing or anything. No need for heat with winter a memory, even when a couple of unseasonably cool days came along like we'd had lately. The smell in there combined ink from the periodicals piled around and grease from the trucks that would roll in and out of here. We four seemed to be alone—no sound of anyone else in the vast chamber.

Sarola ran Independent Newsstand Services. This was only one of several INS warehouses in Manhattan—he covered the entire nation, with his string of warehouses and fleet of trucks—and comic books were the backbone of his business. He distributed girlie magazines, men's adventure rags and low-end paperbacks, too. But he was very much in second place to Newsstand Distribution, Inc., which had the most popular comic-book line in the country (Americana) as well as the best of the slick magazines and paperback companies.

Savor, why don't you, the irony that the two major distributors of the comic books featuring strong-jawed all-American heroes like Wonder Guy, Batwing and Crime Fighter were run in part or in whole by gangsters like Frank Calabria and Vince Sarola. Comic books in which the bad guys the good guys slugged and jugged were thugs not unlike the ones standing behind me right now....

"Been a long time, Jack," Sarola said in his rich baritone.

We were not old pals. I'd encountered him maybe half a dozen times in twenty years. But Sarola had at one time been a partner of the major's, and one of Frank Calabria's top men, who had broken off in the early '40s to start his own rival firm. Calabria, who was a silent partner but a key one in Newsstand Distribution, had allowed this because Sarola was dealing with lower-end, more questionable material that ND did not care to carry.

If you're wondering why gangsters would be involved in magazine distribution, here's a brief history lesson: Calabria became involved as a silent partner in many periodical firms when, *during Prohibition*, those firms decided to buy their paper in *Canada*. Got it?

"Mr. Sarola, a pleasure," I said. "The major thought the world of you."

The major despised Sarola.

"The major was a grand old guy," Sarola said. "The business is much the lesser without him."

Sarola despised the major.

"If I'm not out of line saying," I said, "all it would've taken to get me here was a phone call. Or you could come see us at the office, any time. I'm sure Maggie would be delighted to see you again."

Maggie despised Sarola.

"Well," the gangster said smoothly (and he *was* smooth, no accent, more than passable grammar), "much as I would enjoy that…"

Sarola didn't despise Maggie. He liked strippers.

"…we have a situation here, a problem here, that makes such niceties impossible. A situation, Jack, that is getting worse by the minute. By the second."

"What situation is that, Mr. Sarola?"

"Come on, Jack. It's *Vince*." The brutal face split with a smile. His teeth were perfect—they should have been, for what they cost him. "You're the major's kid, for Chrissake. We go back forever, you and me."

"We do at that, Vince."

Still smiling like a greenish jack-o-lantern, he opened a drawer and got out two water glasses and a bottle of bourbon. "How about a snort, kiddo?"

"No thanks."

"Oh, that's right! You don't *drink*, do you? I admire that. That's rare, a guy who can't handle the sauce has the presence of mind, the goddamn will power, to put it aside…. *Lou!* Get Jack a Coca-Cola from the machine."

Sarola flipped a nickel to Lou, the flat-faced guy, who

trundled off somewhere, slipping between walls of bundles and boxes.

"Coca-Cola all right, Jack? We got Seven-Up, too."

"Coke is fine."

He poured himself three fingers of bourbon. Jim Beam. He had a sip. If he thought that would bother me, he was wrong. True, I was trembling just a little, but it had nothing to do with bourbon.

Then, gesturing magnanimously, he said, "I invited you over to see me, after hours, in private like this..." As if the warehouse were a magnificent mansion. "...because I want you to...*clarify* a couple of things for me."

"Glad to."

He sipped bourbon. "You're buddies with Bob Price at Entertaining Funnies, right? I'm not wrong about that, am I?"

I shrugged. "We're friendly. We're considering doing business with him. Looking at syndicating a *Craze* Sunday page."

His eyes flared and the wide grin flashed. "*There's* a successful book! One million copies a month in a market that's, I won't shit you, Jack, fallen off lately." He sipped more bourbon. "You even went along to that dog-and-pony show with Price, over at Foley Square, didn't you?"

"I did."

"What, just as a friend?"

"Sort of a bodyguard. He's had death threats, and the press can be a pain in the ass."

"*Can't* they, though!" He swirled the deep amber liquid in the glass, stared at it as if reading tea leaves. Almost absently, he said, "Entertaining Funnies is one of ours, you know. So that makes us allies of a sort."

"Of a sort," I granted.

His forehead frowned though he continued to smile. "Then why is it you're giving some of our *other* friends a hard time?"

"What friends?"

He raised a hand and his expression seemed embarrassed, though I didn't buy it. "Afraid I get ahead of myself sometimes, Jack. When I care about something, really care deeply, I do that. You'll have to forgive me."

The flat-faced thug was walking over toward us, his footsteps like gunshots echoing off the cement. He handed me the Coke, which wasn't terribly cold. I thanked him. He said nothing and moved back behind me.

"We dodged a bullet, you might say," Sarola went on, "over at Foley Square. Did you know Bert Levinson went to Europe, just to duck subpoenas? Hell, I thought about doing the same thing myself. I mean, if Kefauver had got wind of my part in this business? Or your friend Frank's?" He meant Frank Calabria, of course. "Why, we'd be up to our ass in federal alligators, get hit with a whole new round of crime hearings, wouldn't that be the shits? And if you think funny books got a bad name *now*, well…" He waved this dismal thought away.

I was still wondering what this had to do with me.

I said, "Well, those senators didn't dig into the distribution end. Probably because it really *was* just a dog-and-pony show. The Republicans have Commies for a whipping boy, the Democrats have comic books. It'll blow over."

"Maybe it *would* have," he said, big eyes small now under the slashes of black. A thick finger pointed at me, like this was my fault, whatever it was that had brought me here.

"But now that this Dr. Frederick bastard's been bumped, who *knows* what merry hell's gonna get stirred up."

I frowned, trying to follow him. "You think Frederick dying is a *bad* thing?"

"If it was suicide, it would be a *beautiful* thing. If it's murder, everybody in the business stands to be screwed over."

"That depends on who did it."

His eyes seemed to see me for the first time, as if up to now he'd been talking to himself. "What do you mean by that, Jack?"

"I mean, if *you* hired it done, Vince...by way of some fancy contract killer who got way too cute in staging the thing...*that* would be bad for business. If it came to light."

His thick upper lip curled into a sneer. "Is that what you think, Jack? That *I* hired it done?"

"No. I don't. It doesn't smell like mob, if you'll forgive the expression."

His head tilted back and he looked down that considerable nose at me. "You're saying I'm a *mobster* now? Why would you slander a legitimate businessman like Vince Sarola?"

Oh Christ. Now he was talking about himself in the third person. Never a good sign.

I said, "I'm saying you didn't have this done. It causes you more trouble in the long run than anything it saves you in the short term. You're right—Dr. Frederick, murdered, could stir things up. He could become a damn martyr."

"Okay," he said. His sigh was like the Big Bad Wolf blowing down a pig's house. "Okay, Jack. I do like your attitude in this respect."

I sipped my Coke. I was feeling less anxious.

Then he said, "So let me get back to where we started." That sounded amiable. This didn't: "Why are you going around giving my friends a hard time?"

I set the Coke on his desk. "I don't follow you, Vince."

"My boys picked you up, coming out of the Entertaining Funnies offices. You led the goddamn badges there, Jack."

I held up a palm. "No, that's not right. The cops were already on their way. I beat Captain Chandler over there, so I could warn Bob and his partner Feldman, and get them ready for what was coming."

His sneer turned into a terrible frown. "Yeah? What about you going over to *Lev's* offices? And threatening Charley Bardwell?"

"I didn't threaten him. If he said that, he's a goddamn liar."

"Then you *didn't* track Pete Pine down, beat the shit out of him, and turn his ass over to your pal Chandler?"

I sat forward. "Vince, this is as straight as it comes—Maggie asked me to look into the doc's murder, because for the good of the business, the thing needs to be cleared up but fast. We at Starr don't want comics getting a black eye any more than you do."

Still that awful smile. "So you decided to make Pete Pine the fall guy? Or maybe Charley Bardwell? Or even your 'friend,' Bob Price?"

I was shaking my head. "There's no 'fall guy' about it. If I can find out who did this, and right away, we can maybe control and contain the bad press. If Pete Pine killed that shrink, so be it. Let the chips fall."

"You're not stitching him up for it?"

"Not him or anybody."

"Not even *me*, Jack?"

"Are you kidding? Do I look suicidal?"

The big brutal face bore no expression at all now. "Some-times, Jack, you never know who's gonna get the blues and throw a rope over a rafter."

"Vince, we're not on opposite sides here. I have no inten-tion of 'stitching' *anybody* up for this kill."

He finished his glass of bourbon, leaned back in his chair and rocked. "So Maggie wants you to clear this up, 'cause it'd be good for business? Like your Uncle *Frank's* business?"

"Calabria's not my uncle."

"You always called him that."

"Everybody calls him that. We have a very small piece of Americana and Calabria's a silent partner in that, as you damn well know, Vince…and he's got a piece of Newsstand Distribution, too, which by the way we own not the smallest slice of, even though the major started the damn business."

His eyes narrowed. "I suppose you and Frank haven't even discussed this thing?"

"What thing?"

"The Frederick kill."

"No, we haven't."

"And you haven't talked to Louis Cohn over at Americana about it, either?"

"No!"

He gestured with an open hand. "You know, if we go under, Newsstand Distribution won't want anything to do with Levinson Publications and Entertaining Funnies. Stuff they print is way too rough for their taste. And if that leaves

Lev's comics and Price's comics without distribution, that puts Americana and Calabria in the catbird seat. You realize that, don't you, Jack?"

"If this Senate hearing, and Frederick's murder, make it so nobody'll do business with you anymore, then you're cooked, yeah. But I have nothing to do with that. Nor does 'Uncle Frank,' at least as far as I know."

I stood.

"Is that all?" I said. "This is a load of horse crap, Vince, and I'm ready to go home."

He shook his head. "You're not."

He lifted a finger and big hands came in and took me by the shoulders and sat me down hard on the wooden chair. The guy with the feathered porkpie hat was behind me and he reached those big mitts around and grabbed me by the elbows and squeezed, holding me into place. The flat-faced guy, with a tiny smile indicating a big love for his work, hit me in the face. My nose didn't break but it began to bleed. Big fists pummeled my midsection and my chest. The guy knew how to give a beating without breaking any ribs and it didn't hurt any more than falling off a two-story building. Right, left, right, left, I was his goddamn punching bag. This went on for about a minute that seemed about five.

Past my assailant, I could see the seated Sarola, just taking in the show dispassionately. Then he raised a hand. This apparently signaled the feather-hat guy holding me to nod to the flat-faced guy hitting me to let up.

"Give him a drink," Sarola said, as if worrying about my health.

The seated gangster handed the Jim Beam bottle across the desk to Lou and as the guy behind me held onto me by my elbows, the flat-faced thug grabbed my face, pushed my head back and, squeezing my lips at the sides like a pimple he was popping, forced open my mouth. He upended the bottle and stuck the snout in and poured the liquid glug-glug-glugging in and I didn't swallow any, not at first anyway, just kept expelling the stuff, as best I could, bubbling it back at him, and the booze went all over the front of me, my suit, my shirt, and some of it did go down my throat, burning as it went. My belly burned, too.

Lou said in a high-pitched voice as flat as his face, "It's empty. Got another bottle, boss?"

Sarola ignored that and said to me, "Here's the thing, Jack —we're gonna have the same conversation we just had, but we're gonna see if a friendly drink hasn't loosened you up some. And if not, we'll try some more good old-fashioned persuasion. We'll beat on you and pour bourbon down your gullet till we believe you. Ready?"

I nodded.

Then I kicked out and caught the desk and propelled myself backward, knocking the guy behind me off balance and the feathered porkpie right off his head. It also caused him to let go of me and I dove to the right, grabbed back and got the chair and hit him with it. In the movies, in bar fights, chairs break into kindling. In a real fight, particularly when it's a nice old solid oak chair like this one, that chair just makes a nice satisfying thud as it smacks into muscle and bone, and the big beefy guy went down, crying out for his mother.

The other thug went for his gun and I kicked him between the legs so hard his eyes rolled back in his head. He went down, too, like he was praying only his clasped hands were on his nuts, and I took the gun from under his arm and whirled and smacked the other guy with it, who was up again, but not for long. Lou's gun was a long-barreled .38 and it had caught my driving companion across the temple and he went down for the count. The other guy was getting up and I kicked him in the head.

He went to sleep, on his back.

I disarmed the now hatless guy, tossing the gun into the darkness; it clunked and didn't go off. Not that I would have given a damn if it did.

Sarola was still behind his desk, but now he was opening a drawer and going for something and it wasn't a bottle of bourbon. I put everything I had into charging that desk, pushing it back, and the desk and Sarola went smacking into the wall of cartons and bundles, which tottered and caved in, unleashing an avalanche of boxes. I scrambled out of the way as a pile of the things came tumbling down until there was no sign of the desk, with only Sarola's feet sticking out from under a heap of boxes, like the witch under Dorothy's house in *The Wizard of Oz*.

It might have killed him, which I wouldn't have lost any sleep over, but I doubted it had. I was hurting from the punches I'd taken, and breathing hard, and bleeding from the nose, but could only smile. The boxes right above where Sarola's feet stuck out were labeled LITTLE LULU and UNCLE SCROOGE.

These comic books were dangerous, all right.

I found an automatic switch on the wall by the big garage door, got in my Kaiser-Darrin, backed out of there, and headed for midtown.

It had been a long time since I'd come home with the

taste of bourbon in my mouth, my clothes smelling like a distillery, and that made me smile, too. Made me grin. Had enough gone down my gullet (as Sarola put it) that I was drunk? As many years as I'd been off the stuff, probably wouldn't take much to put me on my ass.

I had a date with Sylvia and normally would have gone right to her apartment in the Village, but instead went to the Starr Building, parking on the street for a change. Everything was going just hunky-dory till I passed out in the elevator.

CHAPTER ELEVEN

I woke to darkness, and had just a moment or two of panic, since my last memory was collapsing in that elevator. Then the irradiated numbers of my nightstand clock told me not merely what time it was—six-twenty—but *where* I was. I reached into the void past the clock for the bedside lamp and switched it on.

Yellow-tinged light gently illuminated my bedroom, as I sat up, surprised to find myself in pajamas. I ached in my chest and midsection where Sarola's two thugs had worked me over, but less than I'd have imagined. After all, I'd only slept, what? Half an hour since I got home? Funny that I neither remembered getting home nor putting on my pajamas, but I knew I had to really shake a leg, even if that hurt a little. I was supposed to pick up Sylvia at her apartment at seven.

I figured I better grab another shower and shave, before my date, and did so. Then, walking from the bathroom into the bedroom with a towel wrapped around me, I found Maggie sitting on the edge of my bed, facing me.

"What are you doing here?" I asked.

"What are you doing out of bed?" she asked, expressionless.

"Getting ready for my date. I'm supposed to pick Sylvia Winters up at—"

"That was yesterday."

"Huh?"

"You were supposed to pick her up Friday night at seven."

"Right."

"And this is Saturday."

"What? How long did I sleep? What is it, morning?"

"No. Evening. Night. Don't worry about Sylvia. She knows."

"Knows what?"

She stood. "That you took a beating yesterday and are recuperating. Why don't you put something on besides that towel."

"…Okay." I had an uneasy feeling, suddenly, about how I'd got into those pajamas.

"I'll get you some coffee."

"Make it Coke."

"You'll lose your teeth someday, over that sugary swill."

"Coke."

She nodded, and went from the bedroom into the kitchen, the next room down in the boxcar layout of my apartment. I traded the towel for underwear from my dresser, then went to my closet and got my navy gabardine, a trifle heavy for this time of year, but the only suit I owned that had been tailored to hide a shoulder-holstered gun.

And while I may have been disoriented, I knew that, for the time being, I wanted to carry a gun.

But all I had on was the socks and suit pants and t-shirt when Maggie returned with the Coke for me and some coffee for herself.

"I take it you're not going back to bed," she observed.

"Well, considering I've slept almost twenty-four hours," I said, "I just may have had enough of a beauty sleep. Let me finish dressing, then let's talk in the living room."

We did.

For inhabiting the same building, neither of us visited the other's apartment often. But when Maggie did drop by, we normally confined her visit to the living room, where we had entertained Starr Syndicate clients and talent fairly often, the modern furnishings and original comic-art wall hangings providing a proper atmosphere.

I could tell she'd been here a while—the latest book she was reading, *Lord Vanity* by Samuel Shellabarger—was split open face down to its place on the coffee table, with multiple coffee cup rings on the glass and a few crumbs from a sandwich or other snack. Her shoes, little red flats, were under the table, and the pillow on the well-padded black leather couch was positioned for napping, the impression of her head providing further evidence.

She'd been babysitting me. I found that touching if a trifle ridiculous, but would make no wisecrack about it. Sentiment embarrassed her. I took a boxy but comfy black-leather chair, mate to the couch, and sipped my Coke. Unlike the bottle that flat-faced guy gave me back at Sarola's warehouse, this one was nice and cold.

"Bryce found you," she said. "You were unconscious in the elevator when he called it up to take him down."

After five o'clock, the elevator was self-service, the attendant gone, the street door locked.

"Don't tell me which one of you undressed me," I said. "Either way, I'm not sure I could handle it."

"You smelled like you'd been bathing in Jim Beam," she said.

"Good nose," I said. "That's what it was."

"But you didn't fall off the wagon, did you?"

"No. But how did you know that?"

She sipped her coffee, shrugged a shoulder. "You'd clearly been beaten. Your sport coat was bloody and torn, your nose swollen, your eyes black. They still are, a little."

"I noticed when I shaved."

"The front of your clothing had been soaked in booze. Someone tried to pour the stuff into you, didn't they?"

I swigged Coke. "And here I thought I was the detective in the family."

"Dr. Carlson felt you'd had some liquor forced on you, but he doubted it would be enough to cause a...relapse to your former condition."

"You mean, it didn't make me an instant drunk?"

She shrugged both shoulders this time. "Sometimes one drink can do it."

"This wasn't a drink, exactly. It was more like a dose of medicine from a really mean daddy."

"Are you going to tell me what happened?"

I did.

My account upset her enough to cause a rare tightening of the eyes. "Shall we call your friend Captain Chandler?"

I shook my head. "No. If I killed Sarola, dropping that wall of boxes on him, why bother? If Chandler wants me on a manslaughter beef, let him come up with his own damn evidence."

"Is that wise?"

I grunted a laugh, which hurt just a little. "Maggie, odds are that tough old bastard Sarola is still alive. So if I go to the cops and accuse him and his two goons of beating on me, they'll just deny it. And add it up any way you like—it still comes out my word against the three of them."

She nodded. Her ponytail bobbed. Right then I would have given a thousand bucks for her not to be my father's widow. Two thousand.

"Besides," she said, musing aloud, "it just dredges up all

that old history with the major's dealings with the mob."

"Not to mention the various mob factions who are involved in magazine distribution in this town, and our tangential connection to one of them."

I meant Frank Calabria, of course.

"Not to mention that," she said. "May I make a suggestion?"

"I'm impressed you asked first. Sure. What?"

Her eyes were hard and unblinking. "Call your Uncle Frank and tell him what happened. Ask him if he can apply his influence to see that you suffer no repercussions from this Sarola incident."

"That's an excellent suggestion. I might have thought of it myself, when my head cleared, but I appreciate the help."

"How *are* you feeling?"

"A little thick in the tongue and between the ears, but not bad. Did you say Dr. Carlson stopped in?"

She nodded. "He gave you two shots, one for pain, another a sedative. That's why you had the nice long nap."

Carlson was known as the Broadway Kildare. Via house (and apartment) calls, he tended to the health problems of actors, actresses, directors, choreographers, and other creative types, and some of his treatments were not strictly by the AMA rule book.

"I must not have needed hospitalization," I said. "Was I awake when he examined me?"

"More or less."

Maybe I was starting to remember that....

"He said you'd be fine," she said, "but if you have any blood in your urine, give him a shout."

"Don't worry, if I piss blood, I'll scream. And he'll hear it. He's only four blocks from here."

She tucked her legs up under her, like a teenage girl at a slumber party. "Are you up for reporting on the rest of your day? Your yesterday, I mean?"

I said I was, and told her about visiting Charles Bardwell and his monkey at Levinson Publications, and gave her a scaled-down account of my stairwell battle with Bardwell's other monkey, Pete Pine, including how he'd tried to toss Lyla Lamont down the stairs after beating on her.

Maggie's eyes flared. "I swear, we need to insist on a different artist for *Crime Fighter*."

"Well, apparently Lyla's been drawing it lately. Why not hire her? She's been making Pine's deadlines better than she used to her own."

Maggie sighed. "Sometimes I think nobody we have under contract is doing their own work," she said, mildly disgusted. "It's all ghosts, ghosts, ghosts. Case in point, I spoke to an editor at Frederick's publisher the other day."

"Why did you do that?"

"This was before he died on us. I wanted to make sure there were no contractual obligations to the book publisher before we inked a syndication deal for a column. I was right to tell the late doctor he could use an assistant. His editor said, off-the-record, that *Ravage the Lambs* was mostly a ghost job."

"Why, that old windbag! That phony."

"Which reminds me. Your new lady friend, Dr. Winters…?"

"I don't know if I like the way you put that…"

"What are we going to do about her?"

I had several ideas, but didn't feel I needed Maggie's advice in that area.

As if reading my mind, or maybe just my expression, she

said, "What I mean is, we offered her a contract to ghost a column by a dead man."

"Oh. Right."

"Or I should say, a man who is now dead."

I had another swig of Coke. "In all the fuss, I hadn't thought that through. That's a bum deal for her. What do you say we give her a shot at a column like that, anyway?"

"Jack, you know very well the point of the column was just to manipulate Dr. Frederick into laying off our comic-book properties...."

I lifted two palms in surrender. "I know, I know. But it's still not a bad idea, however we happened to come up with it—an advice column by an actual shrink. How about we let her write us, say, three sample columns, and if we don't sign her, offer her a nice kill fee for her trouble."

She thought about that, then nodded once. "Yes. That's a good solution. So...getting back to Friday and what your inquiry came up with...."

I told her about Chandler having the drunken Pine picked up and shipped to Bellevue, as well as my visit to the Entertaining Funnies offices—not just my conversation with Bob Price and Hal Feldman, but the encounter with that would-be Brando of the ink brushes, Will Allison.

"I hate to think that kid had anything to do with Frederick's murder," she said.

"Me, too. But he has the brains and, well, bizarre streak needed to rig up that crazy crime scene. My problem with Pine is that he's not that imaginative. Not that bright."

An eyebrow rose a quarter of an inch over a green eye. "But his bosom buddy *Bardwell* is bright—a clever, nasty man, our Mr. Bardwell."

I snapped my fingers. "That's right! I never thought of that possibility. They could have been in on it together, one of their drunken frolics turned deadly. Bardwell and his man-monkey, making Dr. Frederick pay for assorted indignities."

"I like it," she said, as if she and I were Price and Feldman brainstorming horror story "springboards."

I got to my feet. "Listen, I appreciate what you did here, getting a doc in, looking after me...but I'm fine now. No need for chicken soup."

"You'll stay in? Take it easy?"

"Are you kidding? I'm twenty-four hours late for my date with that hubba-hubba headshrinker down in the Village."

She winced. "Please tell me I didn't hear you use the expression 'hubba-hubba.' "

"Sorry." I lifted her gently by the arm off the couch. "What I meant to say was, I'm gonna call my woo-woo baby and see if she's available at short notice."

At the sound of the word "woo-woo," Maggie did something she rarely did, though God knows I tried hard enough on a regular basis to get that out of her: she laughed.

I walked her to the door and when she was halfway out, she did something else remarkable.

She touched my cheek.

"You be careful, Jack."

"Don't worry, Maggie. I'll take a gun."

"Good," she said, and was gone.

You might consider it an odd choice of restaurants, almost as if we were returning to the scene of the crime.

But Sylvia never did get her nice meal at the Waldorf, as

promised by the late Dr. Frederick, and I decided to make up for that. Anyway, I had no desire to fight the bearded boys, long-haired girls, and gawking tourists for a table at a Village bistro on a Saturday night.

Not that I was springing for the Starlight Roof. I could afford that, marginally, but we'd never get in without a reservation.

The Tony Sarg Oasis was another story, just off the lobby and the hotel's coziest dining spot. Also, I knew the maître d', which—along with a three-dollar tip—got us shown immediately to a table for two. We were seated against a curving wall festooned with funny-animal comics characters, in drunken parade—tipsy turtles, pie-eyed primates, tight tigers, lit lions—as drawn by the cartoonist whose name was on the place.

More cocktail lounge than restaurant, the Oasis offered a limited but tasty menu of sandwiches and Hungarian dishes. A little bandstand of violinists and cellists provided a side dish of Hungarian rhapsodies, a romantic touch in a room largely given to couples, sitting in the cigarette-smoky fog like London lovers on park benches.

Sylvia had forgone her usual Beat Generation sweater-and-slacks combo for a black linen dress with white polka-dots and a matching jacket. Most women in the Oasis wore hats, but not Sylvia, who put her money on the lovely short hairdo, its platinum scythe blade of hair swinging at the edge of her apple-cheeked face. Her lipstick was closer to red than black tonight, but she still kept her makeup on the light side, a little face powder, some mascara. Those deep dark blue eyes needed no help at all, really.

"Feels a little ghoulish," Sylvia said, "coming here."

"That's *goulash*," I said.

We had just ordered. She took my advice and tried the Hungarian specialty of the house.

I shrugged. "It's not like we're taking room service in the doc's suite. The Oasis is just a nice place that I could get us into, last minute."

She was looking past me.

"What is it?" I asked.

"Will you look who's sitting over *there*...."

I glanced across the room. Garson Lehman was alone at a table for two. I didn't see him at first, because a waiter was clearing his dishes away.

"You know that guy, Sylvia?"

Even her smirks were pretty. "Everybody in the Village knows him. He's always giving a lecture on sex or starting up a new magazine. I think he's a big phony."

"No argument here."

"Anyway, I saw him on that *Barray Soiree* show, with your stepmother."

"Oh yeah, that's right."

Our goulash arrived, its wonderful aroma steaming up at us, when suddenly I realized somebody was standing next to our table, hovering, and it wasn't a waiter.

"Jack Starr," Lehman said in that familiar nasal whine, after giving Sylvia a little nod of acknowledgment. "Good evening to you."

He was in a gray suit with a floppy black bow tie, his hair again winging right and left, as if he were about to take flight, his mustache twitching with pleasure at seeing me. I had no mustache, but I guarantee you if I had, it wouldn't have been twitching with delight.

"Mr. Lehman," I said. "Surprised to see you here. I figured

you more for the White Horse Tavern type, or maybe Chumley's."

"There are evenings when you could find me at either," he said pleasantly. "But man does not live by bongos and espresso alone."

"I guess not," I said, much more interested in the goulash than this conversation.

He frowned. "And yet…isn't it ironic that we should meet on these premises?"

"Why is that?"

He glanced upward, whether to heaven or the 35th floor, I couldn't tell you. "The loss of my friend and associate, Werner Frederick. Such a tragedy."

The last time I'd talked to him, he was letting me know how much bigger an expert he was on Any Damn Subject than his late "friend."

"You've obviously just been served your supper," he said, "and I don't mean to intrude. I'll call your office tomorrow and we'll make an appointment."

I frowned up at him. "For what?"

The mustache twitched some more. "Well, perhaps you won't be involved. It's more Miss Starr's bailiwick."

"What is?"

"It's just that…much as I dislike capitalizing on the misfortune of others…with Dr. Frederick gone, you will need someone *else* to write that new column for you."

Oh for Christ's sake….

He nodded to me, the wings of hair bouncing, and started off; then he shot a condescending little glance at Sylvia. "And I can assure you, Mr. Starr, that I would *not* need any writing assistance."

He returned to his table where the waiter brought him the check, which he signed, and I said, "What a pompous jackass."

"I guess he didn't realize," Sylvia said, having a delicate bite of the steamy goulash, "that without Dr. Frederick, there is no column."

I hadn't gotten into this with her yet, so before taking another bite, I said, "Not necessarily."

Her expression was curious and hopeful.

"We'll talk about it later," I said.

And we did, at my apartment, which was her first visit. She passed the test with flying colors, loving the framed funny-page artwork and the Bauhaus furnishings. I do keep a liquor cart and made her a martini, olive and all. Just because you're on the wagon, that doesn't mean you can't still be a good host. And ply attractive females with alcoholic beverages.

Now lest you think there was any quid pro quo going on, let me assure you: my telling Dr. Winters about the chance Maggie was offering her, to try out for an advice column of her own, did not have anything to do with us necking on the couch. Nor did it have anything to do with me turning down the lights, leaving only one modest end-table lamp on its dimmest setting, and unzipping the back of her dress, and discovering that she had the most beautiful full breasts in the world. She had worn no bra, and when she shimmied out of the dress, turned out to be free of panties, as well.

She stood before me like Venus de Milo with arms and said, shyly, "Don't think ill of me. I'm no loose woman. I just don't like the lines that underthings make against my clothes."

"That's a perfectly reasonable policy," I said, as I stared

unabashed at the evidence I'd been seeking, and it had nothing to do with a murder case.

She was, as the saying goes, *a real blonde.*

I was sitting on the couch and then she was sitting on me, and her expression as she ground herself exquisitely into me was dreamy and rapturous, lost in herself, just as I was lost in her, but when she finally came, she was looking at me, those dark blue eyes locked onto mine, where they stayed until our breathing had returned to normal.

After an awkward moment when I had to deal with the pants that were down around my ankles, I walked her into the bedroom, both of us naked now, except for me in my black stag-movie socks.

Earlier, when we'd first got to my digs, I had taken my coat off and she had realized for the first time that I was armed, that the shoulder-holstered .45 (a gift from the major, a relic of the Great War) (the gun, not the major) (well, either way really) had been with us the whole evening, and this seemed to frighten and excite her. Before I took the shoulder sling off, she touched the gun, caressed it gently, tenderly.

I forgot to ask her, later, if that might have had any psychological significance.

So, anyway, we walked naked, hand in hand, into the bedroom. She used the bathroom, then I did, and naked as Lyla Lamont the other day, we climbed into my already-slept-in bed and curled up, spoon-style.

We talked about this and that, and eventually got around to the event that so linked us: the murder of Dr. Frederick. I told her, much as I'd told Maggie (though the previous telling did not involve naked spooning), about the events of Friday after I'd sent her off in that cab outside the Waldorf.

Again, I told the tale of Bardwell and his monkey, and gave her chapter and verse about my wild experience in her native Greenwich Village with Pete Pine and Lyla Lamont, from the stairwell battle to the struggle for my innocence. Told her, also, about visiting the Entertaining Funnies offices, and how Will Allison had sought getaway money from his bosses.

"I just don't think Will is a killer," she said. There was no disclaimer of doctor/patient privacy this time. "He's just a confused, creative boy. He blusters but he isn't violent, not really. He's an oddball in a society that doesn't do well with oddballs."

"I came to the same conclusion. Well, Sylvia...now you know everything I know. Is there a suspect you like?"

And without prompting, without my raising it, she said, "Neither that Bardwell nor his pet drinking buddy, Pine, is capable of this crime individually. But together? I think they might just be up to it."

Finally I got around to giving her a detailed account of my kidnapping and beating at the hands of funny-book-distributing gangsters. Now it's just possible I waited to tell her this until I had time to recover from our previous bout of affection on my front-room sofa. I won't cop to that, but it is possible. Possible that I anticipated her sympathy, that I knew if I milked it right she'd un-spoon and roll over toward me and stroke my wounds, among other things, and I'd have another session with this gorgeous shrink, this time not on a couch.

She was asleep, her lovely naked bottom to me, and I was on my back, staring at a ceiling lost in the darkness of the windowless bedroom. I was half-asleep, doing a sort of inventory of what I'd done and seen over the last several days. Going through the suspect list yet again, trying to think like a psychologist about each one, figuring the most important aspect of solving this crime, even more than motive, was understanding who might be capable of the oddly staged "suicide," with its various bizarre elements.

And that's when it happened. Several small details collided like sparks starting a fire, or maybe two nuclei slamming into a subatomic particle to make a nuclear reaction. In the comics, when this kind of big idea comes to you, a light bulb goes off over the character's head.

Well, this was one of those light bulb moments.

And when I turned on the real light bulb in the lamp by the bed, Sylvia rolled over and looked me with squinty eyes and mussed hair and said, "What is it?"

"You may need to get dressed."

She blinked at me, shook her head a little, worked at getting her eyes to focus. "What? Why?"

"I need to talk to Maggie," I said. "And if she comes down here, it's probably better we both have clothes on."

CHAPTER TWELVE

MEET AN *EXPERT* ON *MURDER!*

The Strip Joint was past legal capacity for this week's edition of the televised *Barray Soiree*. The remote broadcast always pulled a decent crowd, but tonight—just one week after host Harry Barray and guest Maggie Starr had gone a few rounds over the comic-book flap—the usual attendees found the restaurant invaded by a number of special guests personally invited by Maggie...all principal players in the Dr. Werner Frederick murder mystery.

Representing Entertaining Funnies at a table for four were publisher Bob Price, his secretary-cum-fiancee Betty, editor/writer Hal Feldman, and artist Will Allison. Price and Feldman had been questioned and released, although Allison remained a suspect, according to Captain Pat Chandler, who was also in attendance, sharing a table up front with his wife and Dr. Sylvia Winters. And me.

Levinson Publications was represented as well, at a table almost adjacent to its EF rivals, with Charley Bardwell and a garishly attractive honey-headed doll I figured for a call girl, and Pete Pine, seated with a clothed-for-a-change Lyla Lamont, if you could call that form-fitting black sheath "clothed." The couple had apparently kissed and made up, or maybe kicked and made up. The monkey had stayed home —the other monkey, that is. (Publisher Levinson himself, and Mrs. Levinson, remained on European vacation.)

Maggie had invited the two groups of comic-book profes- sionals and—because of the business relationship between

Starr Syndicate and both Levinson Publications and Entertaining Funnies—neither dared decline.

Host Barray had initially balked at doing another show on
comic books, the very next week; but Maggie convinced the
D.J. that the murder of Dr. Frederick was keeping the topic
a hot one. Garson Lehman had agreed to appear again,
essentially subbing for the late Frederick, so tonight's broadcast would be very much a continuation or even a sequel to
last week's.

Sylvia—back in one of her trademark oversized sweater-
and-slacks combos (charcoal this time) was watching me
closely, realizing I was neither making small talk nor adoring
eyes at her. Having spoken with Maggie Saturday night, as
we put the pieces together, the lovely shrink surely felt the
same tension in the cigarette-smoke-tinged air that I did.

She also noticed I was wearing the specially tailored navy
suit again, which concealed my shoulder-holstered .45.

"This is more than just a TV show, isn't it?"

I nodded. "Maggie's got something up her sleeve."

"She doesn't have any sleeves."

Maggie was in a low-cut shimmering green cocktail dress,
indeed sleeveless, with a jeweled rose brooch between her
breasts, a third of which were exposed; those big green eyes
of hers were the same shade as her dress. All that red hair
was piled high, perhaps to distinguish her appearance from
last week's show when it brushed her shoulders. Her makeup
was perfect if heavy, full-throttle war paint for public display, including a beauty mark on her right cheek. Making
her the young-looking ponytailed woman who'd tended my
wounds the other night was damn near impossible.

"Figure of speech," I muttered, in answer to Sylvia's remark about Maggie's lack of sleeves.

She glanced around her. "You say Maggie invited all these familiar faces."

"Yes."

"Aren't they...suspects?"

"That's right."

"*All* of the suspects?"

"Well, most of them. Several couldn't attend. Ennis Williams' mother wouldn't let him come, even if she accompanied him. Even if we sent a car."

Sylvia shrugged. "Well, it is a school night."

"Yeah, he wouldn't want to be tardy to the Blackboard Jungle. Anyway, I'll bet his mama lets him stay up to watch the show."

She frowned as she continued slowly scanning the moodily illuminated restaurant. "Who else is missing?"

"Well, a gentleman in the newsstand distribution business, a certain Vincent Sarola, is in the hospital in traction."

The dark blue eyes swung my way. "That's the man who..."

"Who apparently had a bad fall at home."

"How bad?"

"Broke his collarbone, his left arm and his right leg. *He'll* probably be watching, too, on the television in his private room.... Those waitresses are never going to get to us in time. What would you like?"

She wanted a Manhattan, and I took orders from Chandler and his good-looking wife Marge, then left the couple chatting with Sylvia. At the bar, I ordered up drinks for everybody, gentleman that I am.

The show would go on in less than ten minutes, but the crew guys and gals from WNBC were still checking cables and microphones, a clunky trio of which again sat on the linen-covered table of the booth where Barray was already in position, getting his makeup checked, Maggie and Lehman already seated as well. Right now the room was noisy as half a dozen of Maggie's burlesque queen waitresses in their white shirts, black ties and tuxedo pants threaded through the packed tables taking and delivering final drink orders—no service during the show.

"Jack, I wanted to apologize," somebody said.

I looked to one side, but had to tilt my eyes down some, to see the face that went with the voice.

Diminutive Pete Pine, hair combed, freshly shaved, in a black-flecked tan sport coat and darker brown slacks, was barely recognizable as my stairwell brawler. He'd covered a few bruises with shaving powder, but then so had I. He cleaned up surprisingly well.

"Hi, Pete," I said. "Maggie appreciates you coming."

He looked like he might cry; so many sober drunks do. "You've always been a decent guy to me, Jack. And Maggie's been great. Means a lot to a comic-book hack to land a syndicated strip."

"*Crime Fighter* strip's doing fine. We'll see if this bad publicity hurts us."

"Yeah. But I'm…really sorry about the other day. Hey, you used to be a drinker, right? Maybe you let things get out of hand a time or two, yourself, huh? Maybe you can understand, and cut me some slack, just this once?"

And he held out his hand.

I shook his hand, but then I held onto it, tightening the

grip. "We got no problem, Pete. Not unless I hear you're beating up on Lyla again."

I let go.

He shook his head. "Won't happen. I got on my hands and knees and promised her I'd never lay another angry hand on her. I cried my damn eyes out, like a little kid. Man, when I sobered up I felt *terrible* about it. What kind of guy hits a dame, anyway?"

"My point precisely."

Then Bardwell, who'd been watching Pine and me talk, got up from their table and made his way over with the kind of big grin a used car salesman gives you when you walk onto the lot. The six-four artist/editor, in a maroon sport coat with a gray shirt and darker gray tie, loomed over his little pal—all he lacked was the organ grinder's box.

"Hope you two boys are gettin' along famously now," Bardwell said, placing a hand on his cohort's shoulder.

Pine nodded, smiled nervously.

"Jack, Pete here felt like hell about your little…misunderstanding. When I heard you two guys got into a dust-up, hell, I was beside myself."

I said to Pine, "Give me a second with Charley, would you?"

Pine nodded and, tail tucked between his legs, went back to sit with Lyla.

Bardwell's big toothy smile seemed vaguely threatening. "Did you want something, Jack?"

I didn't smile. "Charley, I know you're the one who sicced Sarola and his goons on me the other day. I left your office and you called him."

"Jack, that's crazy."

"No, it's exactly what you'd do. It's exactly what you *did*. Now here's how it's gonna be, Charley. Starr will keep doing business with you as long as the *Crime Fighter* strip holds its list of papers. The second it drops off, *it* gets dropped."

The confidence had gone out of that smile, like air from a punctured tire. "Well, there's *always* ebb and flow with a comic strip...."

"Maggie and I'll make a reasonable decision about it. We won't go off half-cocked. But if Vince Sarola or any of his boys look at me cross-eyed, I will not only deal with *them*, Charley, I will come find *you*."

"Is that right?"

I unbuttoned the navy suit coat, which hung open just enough to reveal the .45 in the shoulder holster. "And, Charley, I just *might* go off half-cocked."

His smile had turned sick. He wasn't at all sure of himself as he said, "You don't scare me, Jack. You're no tough guy."

A hand settled on his shoulder, and Captain Chandler said, "I'd be careful if I were you, Charley. Jack won a Silver Star in the war, y'know. I doubt he'd have much compunction about punching a round or two into you."

Bardwell, who'd been questioned by Chandler about the Frederick killing, knew just who the captain was. And all the bluster drained out of him. So did the blood from his face. He swallowed, nodded, and got back to the Levinson table.

"Compunction, huh?" I said. "Pretty big word for somebody who flunked the inspector exam."

"I liked how I followed it up with 'punching.' Nice ring to it, don't you think?"

"Thanks for not mentioning I won the Silver Star stateside."

I'd got it as an M.P. when there had been a break-out at the P.O.W. camp in Oklahoma where I was stationed.

"The Nazis didn't make it past Tulsa, as I recall," Chandler said.

We had our backs to the bar, watching the final frantic preparations being made for the broadcast.

He asked, "Were you going to tell me about Sarola?"

"Tell you what?"

"Vince claims he fell off his roof putting up a TV antenna."

I laughed. "Maybe he did."

"Word on the street is you dropped a ton of funny books on his ass."

"You always hear about this 'word on the street,' but where does it come from, anyway?"

"In this instance, Jack, I would guess from one of the two bozos you beat to shit telling some goombah buddy, and word got around."

"On the street."

"Yeah. On the street."

"Never."

"What?"

"That's when I was going to tell you."

The drinks were ready and I let Chandler convey them back to the waiting women, so I could make a stop at the Entertaining Funnies table.

"Thanks for coming," I said, leaning in between Price and Feldman. "Should be as entertaining as one of your funnies."

Price gazed up at me, eyes wide behind his dark-rimmed glasses, his manner animated. "Maggie's *up* to something, isn't she? Hal and I were talking, and we figure—"

"Yeah," Feldman said, talking over Price, "we figure that—"

I raised a hand to shush them. "Boys, thanks, but no spring-boarding is needed. Maggie writes her own stuff. With maybe a little help from me."

Will Allison, no motorcycle leathers this time, just a light-blue suit and tie, touched my coat sleeve as I was about to go. His dark eyes were painfully earnest as he stared up at me. "Mr. Starr?"

"Hiya, Will."

"I know you put a good word in for me with Captain Chandler. I just wanted to thank you. I hated what Dr. Frederick stood for, but I didn't have anything to do with his...with what happened. I hope you *know* that."

I patted his shoulder. "Will, this'll all be over soon."

"That sounds a little ominous."

"It may be for somebody."

His grin was shy. "Anyway, thanks. Let me know if there's something I can do to repay you."

"Well, there's two things. First, you can make an appoint-ment to see us next week so we can discuss doing a strip with you."

"What! You're kidding...."

"No, come see us. And the other thing you can do?"

"Yeah?"

"I collect comic art. Pick me out a nice EF page."

"Gee, Mr. Starr, I can't do that."

He really did say "gee."

"Why's that, Will?"

He nodded toward the plump bespectacled publisher. "Mr. Price keeps all the original art. He says he paid for it and he's keeping it—we don't get it back. But I tell you what—if

I wind up doing a strip for Starr, you can have the first Sunday page."

I laughed. "That's the best bribe I've had since..." Well, since Lyla Lamont pranced around in a red beret and the altogether otherwise, but we didn't need to get into that. "...in some time."

A floor director in a headset called for quiet, waving around a clipboard like he was guiding a plane in. Rather than push through the crowd to get to my chair next to Sylvia, I returned to the nearby bar, where a stool at the end waited. Anyway, it gave me a great view past the big blocky camera.

I sat on the edge of my stool, sipping at a rum and Coke (minus the rum), as Harry Barray welcomed his audience at home and here at the Strip Joint. Then the big blond puffy-featured disc jockey began with a brief editorial, directed at the camera.

"Last week we discussed the comic-book controversy that has been sweeping the land," he said, his voice amplified in the room, giving his words extra weight. "Parents are concerned about the violence and horror that drench the pages of these oh-so-unfunny funny books. Churches, schools and PTAs have burned heaps of this trash, which even now litters our nation's newsstands, drugstores and candy shops. On last week's *Soiree*, I suggested that 'adults only' tags might be affixed to these tasteless periodicals."

By the way, Barray was wearing a red-and-black plaid blazer that was at least as tasteless as any comic book I ever saw.

"Such labeling would be a sensible first step in the battle

to safeguard the innocence of our children. This past week, two events occurred that have brought this battle to a boil."

Can you boil a battle?

"A patriotic group of Congressmen," Barray was saying, "held a hearing in our city and exposed the shallow, venal, corrupt attitudes and practices of those whose business it is publishing this trash."

I glanced at Price and Feldman, the former reddening, the latter scowling. At the Levinson table, Charley Bardwell was whispering in the call girl's ear and Lyla Lamont was playing with Pete Pine's hair.

"Perhaps the star of that hearing," Barray went on, "was the psychiatrist who brought the comic-book problem to the attention of American moms and dads, pastors and teachers. With his book on the subject about to be published, Dr. Werner Frederick is rightly the hero of the hour. But he cannot enjoy that status—late last week, as many of you know, he was *murdered*…in a wicked attempt to make it appear he'd taken his own life. Though the police have withheld key aspects of their investigation, inside sources indicate that the very murder itself imitated a violent act depicted in a comic book."

Now, finally, Barray turned to his guests. "We've asked back two experts with opposing views on the subject of comic-book violence—Maggie Starr, the President of the Starr Syndicate…which distributes comic-strip versions of several popular comic-book heroes…and Garson Lehman, noted critic of comic books in his own pioneering book, *The Velvet Fist*. Garson, thank you for again taking part in the *Soiree*."

"My pleasure, Harry." The little man's mouth twitched a

smile under his mustache. He wore another tweedy jacket with a sweater and shirt beneath, his hair in its typical winged formation.

"You were a colleague of Dr. Frederick's, I believe," the D.J. said. "In fact, you helped research *Ravage the Lambs*."

"I did indeed. If I am not being too bold, I would say I contributed mightily to that work, and with the doctor now a martyr to this cause, I am prepared to step in and step up and continue the good fight."

Maggie said, "You're much too modest, Mr. Lehman."

Barray's frown was almost imperceptible—Maggie was supposed to wait for his prompting, for her *turn*, not just jump in as if this were a real conversation and not a staged one.

"Well," Lehman said, smiling uneasily, "that's *kind* of you, Miss Starr…Maggie…and please, we're friends here, I hope —I'm 'Garson.' "

"Thank you, Garson," she said with a nod and a smile.

"But," he went on in his pinched nasal way, "I would never try to claim credit from Dr. Frederick. He's the man the world associates with the anti-comic-book cause, and I am happy to be his standard bearer."

"In my view," Maggie said, touching a breast where pink flesh met green satin, "you deserve much more credit. It's true, isn't it, that Dr. Frederick—while an articulate speaker, and a dogged researcher—was not much of a wordsmith?"

Lehman smiled again, still uneasy. "Well, perhaps. And I *did* help him assemble his book. After all, he did credit me in his acknowledgments. Going so far as to thank me, saying, 'without whom this book would not have been possible.' "

"And it wouldn't have," Maggie said, "because you wrote it."

Lehman looked as if she had slapped him. Barray's slack-lipped gaping stare spoke wordlessly for itself.

She said, "*Ravage the Lambs* was an expansion of an article about Frederick's research and theories that you wrote for *Collier's* under your own name. You 'ghosted' Dr. Frederick's book, as we say in the business."

Finally Barray managed, "Miss Starr, this is a *serious* accusation…"

"It's not an accusation," she said cheerfully. She glanced at Barray. "It's simply giving credit where credit is due. Mr. Lehman…Garson…is an extremely clever man. But he's human."

"Well," Lehman sputtered, obviously getting worked up, "of *course* I'm human."

"Human," Maggie agreed. "And he makes mistakes. Just Saturday evening he made two, in front of my stepson, Jack Starr…vice-president of the Starr Syndicate. Can we swing the camera around? He's there at the end of the bar."

The cameraman complied, wheeling the big boxy affair toward where I perched on my bar stool and, with its glass eye looking at me, I smiled and waved. The camera returned to its former position. My guess would be the cameraman tightened his shot to get a closer look at Maggie.

Who was saying, "Jack and Dr. Sylvia Winters happened to be dining at the Waldorf at the same time as you, Garson. Which I'm sure you'll recall, yes?"

Irritated, the little man nodded, the wings of his hair bobbing. "Though I fail to see what relevance that might have…."

"Now, Sylvia Winters is a doctor of psychology. She has several patients in the comic-book field who happen to have business relationships with the Starr Syndicate. That's how

Dr. Winters came to our attention. You see, we had approached Dr. Frederick about doing an advice column for us, in the Abigail Van Buren vein, but with a psychoanalytical twist. Nothing to do with comics, mind you, but Dr. Frederick, as a national figure, had become something of a star."

Barray said, "Maggie, please—we're getting off the topic, I'm afraid…"

"No. We're right on the topic. You see, just a week ago it was Mr. Lehman who planted the seed of the idea for Dr. Frederick doing a column. Right here in this restaurant. You see, after last week's broadcast, Mr. Lehman pitched a column of his *own* to us…isn't that right, Garson?"

"It is," he said, defiant and confused. "And later I came to your office to follow up on my proposal only to find out you'd already offered a similar column to Dr. Frederick."

"You did and you didn't," she said.

Barray said, "Did and…didn't?"

Maggie's smile oozed patience. "Dr. Frederick was already dead that morning, when Mr. Lehman came around to 'follow up' on his column idea. Garson only pretended not to know that Frederick had been offered a contract. Pretended disappointment that we'd taken his idea and given it to his colleague. Of course, Mr. Lehman also came to us, in part, to establish a sort of alibi. To be in our offices *before* the doctor's body was discovered."

"You are mistaken, Miss Starr," Lehman insisted stiffly. "I knew nothing of Werner doing a column for you."

"Oh but you did. Saturday night, you looked right at Dr. Winters and told Jack that if we were to hire you for the column…now that Dr. Frederick was dead…*you* would not need a ghost."

The Village's favorite expert swallowed. "So? What does that prove?"

"That you murdered Frederick, though there's more to indicate as much."

Like the dead doctor, silence hung in the room.

"You could only know that Dr. Winters had been hired to do the writing on Dr. Frederick's column…a column that *should* have been yours, in your view…if the doctor *himself* had told you."

"That's a lie," Lehman said, sputtering again. "You told me about the Winters woman in our meeting!"

"No. I didn't. We keep such things very quiet in the syndication business—most confidential. You don't advertise that the name on a column or comic strip isn't that of the actual author or artist. And it was a decision we had only made the day before you came to see us. At the Harlem clinic, the night before his murder, Dr. Frederick told Jack and Dr. Winters that he'd already had one of his researchers check up on her—that researcher was you, Mr. Lehman."

Lehman struggled to find words but nothing happened.

She went on: "And the other mistake you made…a small one, really, something that would very likely have come to light anyway…was signing the check at the Waldorf restaurant. Jack saw you do that, Garson. Which means, you *live* at the Waldorf, don't you?"

Lehman said, "So what if I do? I worked closely with the doctor. He needed me nearby."

"And you probably had a key to his suite, as well. Certainly inside access to what would be the crime scene. You are so very well known as a Greenwich Village denizen, one of its eccentric resident 'experts,' that it never occurred to anyone that you might be residing elsewhere. Of late, at the Waldorf."

"It is no crime to live at the Waldorf," Lehman managed.

"Well, the rates are certainly criminal. The other aspect of this murder is, appropriately, psychological. There are a number of good suspects for the murder of Dr. Werner Frederick—many seated in this very audience. But only you possessed the clever, even arcane turn of mind that would come up with a layered scheme for murder. Was the body strung up purposely too high for the chair the victim supposedly stepped off? No matter. More important is the muddying of the waters that you provided by piling bucket after bucket of Waldorf ice-machine cubes at the foot of the hanging dead man, opening the doors onto the unseasonably cool night as well, all to disguise and cloud the time of death. As the real author of *Ravage the Lambs*, you knew the precise comic book with the ice-block method of suicide that could indicate the killer was a comic-book reader who was, at once, avenging himself on the troublesome anti-comic book crusader, and borrowing a homicide technique from the pages of one of those very comic books… conveniently left on the top of a pile of comics on Dr. Frederick's desk."

"This is outrageous," Lehman said. "It is libel!"

"Slander, actually," Maggie said, "if it were false. Everything I've said can be proved. Under official questioning, Frederick's editor and publisher will have to reveal that you were the actual author of *Ravage the Lambs*. Jack, Dr. Winters and I will testify as to the timing and secrecy concerning her role as the doctor's ghost writer on the column, and you yourself admit you live at the Waldorf and had access to the suite. You will be fingerprinted for comparisons to prints found on that comic-book cover. And a police canvass of Waldorf employees and guests should come up with witnesses who saw you plundering ice machines on, how many floors?"

He moved quickly. Whether he drew the little automatic from his pocket, or whether it had been in his hand under the table for some time, no one would ever know. But he had it now, and he jammed it in Maggie's throat.

"You are a meddlesome bitch, Maggie Starr," he said.

With the snout of the weapon dimpling her throat, Maggie betraying no emotion as he did so, the self-proclaimed expert stared at the camera eye.

"I indeed wrote *Ravage the Lambs*. I indeed had the idea for the column that this woman gave to the very man who had become famous on my back, on my work. And, yes, I killed that pompous bag of gas, with pleasure and a rope. And now, you people...*you people!*...get up from those tables and clear a path because Miss Starr is my passport."

I had stepped off the stool and now I got Maggie's eyes. The lights were bright but somehow she looked through them at me and she narrowed her gaze in what I took to be permission.

Lehman was screaming at them now. "Move! *Move!* Make a path! *Make way!*"

And people were getting up and tables and chairs were moving and scraping and glasses were falling over and general chaos seemed about to reign, Barray himself for once backing away from camera view, hands in the air, as if this were a stick-up.

Lehman shoved the table over, the microphones flying, then clunking, tablecloth slipping to the floor like a lazy ghost, and the little wild-eyed mustached man slipped behind Maggie as they stepped off the small platform on which the booth sat, the gun snout poking her throat. From the front, he was blocked by her, she was tall, he was small, and had to reach up to keep the little automatic in her neck.

But I had a side view.

Garson Lehman knew a lot of things. He was an expert, remember? He knew that he could screw up the time of death with cold. But he didn't know about lividity, for example, and he didn't know, apparently, that a bullet to the head would shut him off like a switch and there would be no pulling the trigger of the gun in Maggie's throat, not when I shot him in the head, which I did, the sound so loud, so cannon-like, that damn near everybody in the room screamed.

But I didn't.

And Maggie didn't, either.

She just shifted to one side as the stringless marionette that was Garson Lehman dropped to the floor, leaving the inside of his head and all the brilliant things in it dripping down a framed *Wonder Guy* comic-strip above the booth where he'd recently sat. He was face down, a limp rumpled little figure, his hair still like wings trying to fly off his head, where the gaping gory exit wound represented the kind of horror you could only see in real life.

Chandler was coming up, and Sylvia, too, but I holstered the gun and went over to Maggie and put my arm around her. She smiled at me.

"Pretty decent shot, huh?" I said, over the building crowd commotion.

"I thought maybe you missed," she said. "I mean, you always wanted to be president of Starr, didn't you?"

"Not *that* bad," I said. "Anyway, I was just trying to make a point."

"Which is?"

"It's not comics that are violent. It's TV."

The death of Dr. Werner Frederick only served to create more interest in *Ravage the Lambs*, which became forever the symbol of the attack on comic books, initially a key source for those "proving" the evils of comics, and later a much condemned and even derided work of spurious research, preposterous hyperbole, and ridiculous theorizing.

Latter-day reappraisals aside, the short term was a big win for the late psychiatrist and for the Senate hearing he'd prompted. By 1956, two-thirds of comic books had disappeared from the racks, and dominant among those remaining were a diminished Americana line and Dell Comics, noted for wholesome titles like *Little Lulu* and various Walt Disney fare.

Various laws in assorted states, including New York, made it illegal to put such words as "crime," "horror" or "terror" in a comic-book title. A self-censoring group of publishers created the Comics Code, which had similar restrictions on such words appearing on covers. The industry's own restrictions were tougher than the Hays Office on the movies or even the FCC over the airwaves.

Ironically, the first organizer of the self-censoring group was Bob Price, who walked out of the second meeting, realizing the organization he began would surely put him out of business.

Which it did not quite do. Price and Feldman had barely

survived two failed attempts to adapt to this new anti-comics world, first a new Entertaining Funnies line that eschewed the now forbidden subjects of crime and horror for historically based titles (*Pirates*, *Knights*, *Flying Aces*) and contemporary topics (*Medicine*, *Newsman*, *Psychiatry*) aimed at teens and adults. Wearing the now familiar white stamp of the Comics Code of America, the titles sputtered and died after a few issues. So did magazine format versions of EF's crime and horror titles, with text illustrating art sans speech balloons, like Hal Foster's *Prince Valiant*—not exactly comics and thus skirting the various bans. But these, too, were noble failures.

What saved Price's bacon, and kept a lot of their artists alive in a marketplace where former comic-book artists tended to wind up sacking groceries or parking cars, was *Craze*.

The anti-comics controversy had barely grazed the popularity of the zany comic book, which sold big numbers even when slightly watered down by the Comics Code. The failed magazine format proved ideal for *Craze*, which grew more and more popular in its slick new guise, and for the rest of his very successful career, Bob Price was a publisher with a single—but enormously popular—title.

The *Craze* comic strip never happened because, initially, the Entertaining Funnies staff was just trying to stay alive in the witch-hunt aftermath of the Foley Square hearing. Then all their energy got channeled into converting the title from comic book to slick-cover magazine. The actual creator of *Craze*, Harold Kertzweil, quit after the first few issues of the new magazine version, demanding half-ownership in the title. Price fired Kertzweil or maybe he quit, but at any rate, soon Hal Feldman was Bob's second-in-command again, taking over as editor of *Craze*. The two survivors of the comics war grew old and rich together.

As for the talented Will Allison, he went to work as an assistant and sometime ghost on the detective strip *Nick Steele* after the death of its creator, Ray Alexander. Eventually he took over a secret agent strip, also created by Alexander, for King Features. He never did work for Starr, but he did give me a nice original.

Soft-spoken, handsome, charismatic, Will Allison became a favorite among the fans who celebrated EF Comics as perhaps the greatest comic books of all time. Virtually all of EF's talented writers and artists lived to enjoy their superstar status among several new generations of fans. *Tales from the Vault* even spawned theatrical films as well as a popular HBO television series, more violent and far sexier than the original comics had been. Doc Frederick must have been twirling in his grave, which considering how many rotting corpses walked through that TV show, made a weird kind of sense.

Harry Barray lost his D.J. job when rock 'n' roll took hold, but held down a talk show till his death in the 1970s, due to cirrhosis of the liver, which could easily have been my fate, but I never did fall off the wagon. I have no idea what became of that kid Ennis Williams; with its founder dead, the Lafargue Clinic in Harlem was gone by 1956. In a way, Frederick's good work died with him while his bad work lingered on.

Lyla Lamont quit comics and became a fashion illustrator, though she, too, was discovered by later generations of comic-book fans, celebrated as one of the handful of great female cartoonists, who had managed to make a mark in what was then a man's world. And *Miss Fortune*, belatedly, achieved the status of a classic comic strip.

Perhaps you followed the popular column "Ask Dr. Sylvia," which was in seven hundred papers at its peak. It ran thirty years, and for many decades I remained friends—and sometimes more—with the lovely psychologist.

Vince Sarola's shotgunned body was found in the trunk of his car in Queens in 1955, and his distribution company, Independent Newsstand Services, like the Harlem clinic without its leader, soon went belly up. Whether my "Uncle" Frank had anything to do with that, I do not know, nor do I wish to. But in its absence, rival Newsstand Distribution, of which Calabria had a piece, flourished.

Distribution problems conspired with the Comics Code to make titles like *Fighting Crime* and *Crime Fighter* untenable, and Bert Levinson closed up shop in '56. Charley Bardwell, always a clever guy, became a graphics artist for NBC, working there till 1972, when he died of a heart attack. I don't know what became of his monkey.

Well, not the actual monkey. The fate of Bardwell's other sidekick, I followed in the papers, and not in the funny pages.

After the hearing, papers dropped the *Crime Fighter* strip by the score, and Starr folded it. After Levinson stopped publishing comic books, Pete Pine's boozing got so out of hand that even his longtime buddy Bardwell dropped him. Nobody in the now much smaller comic-book market wanted Pine's stuff, though he did scrounge out an existence drawing sleazy sex gag cartoons for low-end men's magazines.

He did, however, have a girlfriend with a job with a top advertising agency. They both drank heavily, and argued a lot, mostly about why Pine refused to marry her (seems he'd been married twice before and it hadn't worked out). In September 1958, they went on a binge together in the girl-friend's apartment in a Gramercy Park residential hotel. They drank for days on end, and fought violently. Pine hit her with an iron, among other things, before pushing her out the fourteenth floor window.

The papers made a lot of it—"Editor of *Fighting Crime* Comic Murders Ad Woman in Hotel Tryst"—but the story would have gotten more play a few years earlier, at the peak of the anti-comics movement. Particularly if Pine had been the guy who drew the falling-woman cover that had got Kefauver so riled up at the Foley Square hearing.

What a hell of an irony, if that cover had been one Pine drew for Bardwell. But it wasn't. Instead it was a *Suspense Crime Stories* from Bob Price and Entertaining Funnies. And Price probably didn't even pick up on the resonance when he read the Pine story in the papers. He was too busy making a mint, sticking a grinning idiot on the covers of *Craze*.

As for Pine, he did a modest three years in Sing Sing before getting out and finding no work as an artist. He became a short-order cook at a diner, where two old prison "pals" picked him up one night, seeking repayment for loans; when Pine couldn't make good, they shot him in the head and dumped him off the New Jersey turnpike.

That was 1961, the year Marvel Comics made a splash with *Fantastic Four* and *Spider-Man*, revitalizing the comic-book industry, just in time for Pete Pine to miss it.

A TIP OF THE FEDORA

This novel, despite some obvious parallels to events in the history of the comics medium, is fiction. It employs characters with real-life counterparts as well as composites and wholly fictional ones.

Unlike other historical novels of mine—the Nathan Heller "memoirs," the Eliot Ness series, the "disaster" mysteries, and the *Road to Perdition* saga—I have chosen not to use real names and/or to hew religiously to actual events. This is a mystery in the Rex Stout or Ellery Queen tradition, with a dollop of Mickey Spillane, and real-life conflicts have been heightened and exaggerated while others are wholly fabricated. Characters reminiscent of real people, in particular professionals in the comic-book field, are portrayed unflatteringly at times, because they are, after all, suspects in a murder mystery.

While I invite readers—particularly comics fans—to enjoy the *roman à clef* aspect of *Seduction of the Innocent*, I caution them not to view this as history but as the fanciful (if fact-inspired) novel it is.

This novel centers upon the comic-book controversy of the 1950s, and a number of characters here have obvious parallels to real people.

The murder victim, Dr. Werner Frederick, is a fictional character drawing heavily upon the very real Dr. Fredric Wertham, whose anti-comics crusade indeed earned him public death threats from comic-book artists, although none were carried out. Frederick is not intended to be the real Wertham, rather the *idea* of Wertham, among professionals and fans alike. It should be noted that Wertham made important contributions to the Civil Rights Movement that have been unfortunately if understandably overshadowed by his anti-comics zealotry.

Others in these pages have similarly obvious real-life counterparts—Bill Gaines and Al Feldstein are represented by Bob Price and Hal Feldman, Al Williamson by Will Allison, Charles Biro by Charles Bardwell, Bob Wood by Pete Pine, and so on. Despite any parallels, these are melodramatic caricatures not intended to represent the real people.

That said, Charles Biro was known by colleagues for frequent boozing and womanizing in the company of Bob Wood, the former working with a pet monkey on his shoulder, the latter with an alcohol monkey on his back. Wood did commit a murder similar to the one outlined in the final pages of this novel.

The lovely Tarpe Mills, creator of *Miss Fury*, posed for herself in the nude with no shyness about doing so in front of male colleagues—a fact confirmed to me some years ago by Golden Age comic-book writer Spillane. The character Lyla Lamont, however, does not represent Mills, and is instead a fanciful composite of *Miss Fury*'s creator and several other women who wrote and drew comic books in the 1940s and '50s. An excellent collection of *Miss Fury* (2011) has been assembled by my friend Trina Robbins, herself a noted cartoonist and writer (*Great Women in Comics*, 2001).

Garson Lehman has a vague basis in Dr. Wertham's real-life associate, Gershon Legman, who was rumored to have ghosted Wertham's famous anti-comics screed, not coincidentally also entitled *Seduction of the Innocent* (1954). Legman's book *Love and Death* (1949) did precede Wertham's more famous one in its criticism of comics. Legman was a collector of, and commentator upon, erotica, and his point (better than any Wertham came up with) was that mass culture wrongly censored sex while giving violence a pass. Just as Dr. Wertham was not a murder victim, Legman was not a murderer.

Dr. Sylvia Winters is minorly inspired by Dr. Lauretta Bender, who defended comic books as cathartic reading material for children. Harry Barray has a similar minor basis in radio/TV personality Barry Gray, who spoke out against comics, and in the mid-'50s had a talk show broadcast remotely from a Manhattan steak house. That talk show was once interrupted by a comic-book artist in the audience crying foul. Neither portrayal intends to depict the real people.

Frank Calabria, an off-stage presence in this novel (who appears in the first Jack and Maggie Starr mystery, *A Killing in Comics*, 2007) is based on real-life gangster Frank Costello. Vince Sarola is a fictional character, as is Ennis Williams, although Dr. Frederic Wertham did run the Lafargue Clinic in Harlem, as outlined in a March 1948 *Collier's* article, "Horror in the Nursery," written by future famous film critic, Judith Crist. The article actually did reprehensibly substitute staged photos of upscale white children in the place of the doctor's impoverished ghetto patients.

My longtime research associate, George Hagenauer, provided a huge pile of contemporary articles from magazines and newspapers, reflecting the hysteria of the anti-comic-book movement of the '50s. Countless small details about

Greenwich Village and other Manhattan locations were culled from various Internet sources—for the record, the Village Gateway is suggested by the Village Gate, which hadn't quite opened for business at the time of this novel.

Four books in particular were of great help in the writing of *Seduction of the Innocent*, and for anyone interested in the history of comic books—or, for that matter, popular culture in America in the 20th Century—I recommend all four highly.

David Hajdu's *The Ten-Cent Plague* (2008) is the definitive work on the comic-book "witch hunt," beautifully written and painstakingly well-researched (although I must be forgiven for pointing out that the *Dick Tracy* strip began in 1931, not 1929). Hajdu's account of the Senate hearing at Foley Square provided the major reference for the chapter on that event in this novel. Much of what is said in that sequence reflects what really was said at the hearing. I have used the real names of the senators.

A broader look at the development of comic books in the 1940s and '50s, *Men of Tomorrow: Geeks, Gangsters and the Birth of the Comic Book* (2004) by Gerard Jones, was similarly helpful. Like Hajdu, Jones has written a definitive work—an entertaining, informative examination of the early days of comic books.

While homicidal cartoonist Bob Wood rates space in the above two books, my friend Denis Kitchen's introduction to the collection *Crime Does Not Pay* (2001) tells the whole grisly story. Kitchen recounts the full, fascinating history of Lev Gleason's comic book company, where Wood and Charles Biro created (with the help of other writers and artists) the lively, brutal crime comics anthologized in that volume.

A lavishly illustrated history of EC Comics, *Foul Play!* (2005) by Grant Geissman, provided much background for this novel as well as photographs that brought the people, their surroundings, and the times to life in a manner unbelievably helpful to a historical novelist. While I was only able to explore a handful of EC's legendary creators here, Geissman brings their whole world to life.

As a writer of comic strips and books myself, I have had the privilege over the years of meeting many EC artists and writers, including Al Feldstein, Harvey Kurtzman, William Gaines, and my favorite comic-book writer/artist, Johnny Craig.

Other books on the history of comic books that I consulted included *The Horror! The Horror!* by Jim Trombetta (2010); *The Mad World of William M. Gaines* by Frank Jacobs (1972); and *Seal of Approval: The History of the Comics Code* by Amy Kiste Nyberg (1998). My thanks to these authors, as well.

As a child and later as a teenager, I read the Muscatine (Iowa) Public Library copy of Wertham's *Seduction of the Innocent* any number of times. Like many Baby Boomer comic-book fans—long before I knew of the existence of other fans like me—I used Wertham's book not as a guide to the comics I should be avoiding, but the ones I should be looking for. As indicated in this novel, the original *Seduction of the Innocent* is extensively illustrated with the most violent and/or sexual off-the-wall, out-of-context panels possible. I read it again, once or twice, over the years, and I frankly did not bother doing so in preparation for my own book of the same title. Wertham's *Seduction* is quoted at length in Hajdu and Jones, which was sufficient for my purposes.

Again, I have leaned upon *New York: Confidential!* (1948) by Jack Lait and Lee Mortimer for Manhattan color. Other New York background came from *No Cover Charge* (1956), Robert Sylvester; *New York Night: The Mystique and its History* (2005), Mark Caldwell; and *It Happened in Manhattan* (2001), Myrna Katz Frommer & Harvey Frommer. Helpful, too, was *Live Television: The Golden Age of 1946-1958 in New York* (1990). I also made use of the article "The Village" by John Wilcock, *Rogue* magazine, July 1961.

The Jack and Maggie Starr mysteries were conceived as a trilogy. That's not to say I might not return to the characters, should readers indicate a desire I do so, rather to indicate I initially had three topics in the history of comics that I wanted to explore. Those topics were the creation of *Superman* by two teenagers from Cleveland, who got screwed over in the process (*A Killing in Comics,* 2007); the feud between two of my favorite syndicated-strip cartoonists, *Li'l Abner* creator Al Capp and *Joe Palooka* creator Ham Fisher, resulting in the latter's suicide (*Strip for Murder,* 2008); and the McCarthy-era comic-book witch hunt and its chief organizer, Dr. Frederic Wertham (*Seduction of the Innocent,* 2012). But the previous publisher of the series opted not to continue after the first two, leaving the trilogy hanging. Editor Charles Ardai of Hard Case Crime came to the rescue, allowing me to complete the third book in what was conceived as a left-handed history of comics and an affectionate tribute to Rex Stout, Archie Goodwin and Nero Wolfe. Thank you, Charles.

Thanks also go to my longtime comics collaborator, cartoonist Terry Beatty, who again helped incorporate graphic novel elements into this work of prose, this time around perfectly capturing the EC Comics feel.

Thanks also go to my agent and friend, Dominick Abel, for his continuing support and hard work; and my wife Barbara, who read and edited this novel chapter-by-chapter, despite being in the midst of her draft of our latest "Barbara Allan"-bylined collaborative novel.

The Final Crime Novel from
THE KING OF PULP FICTION!

DEAD
STREET

by **MICKEY SPILLANE**

**PREPARED FOR PUBLICATION BY
MAX ALLAN COLLINS**

For 20 years, former NYPD cop Jack Stang has lived with the memory of his girlfriend's death in an attempted abduction. But what if she didn't actually die? What if she somehow secretly survived, but lost her sight, her memory, and everything else she had…except her enemies?

Now Jack has a second chance to save the only woman he ever loved—*or to lose her for good.*

ACCLAIM FOR MICKEY SPILLANE:

"One of the world's most popular mystery writers."
— The Washington Post

*"Spillane is a master in compelling you to
always turn the next page."*
— The New York Times

"A rough-hewn charm that's as refreshing as it is rare."
— Entertainment Weekly

"One of the all-time greats."
— Denver Rocky Mountain News

**Available now at your favorite bookstore.
For more information, visit
www.HardCaseCrime.com**